The Fifth Skull

A HISTORICAL NOVEL OF THE CIVIL WAR
AND THE AMERICAN WEST

To Milton Strickland,
With best wishes.
Jerrell T. Gorr

Also by Terrell T. Garren

THE SECRET OF WAR
A Dramatic History of Civil War Crime
in Western North Carolina

MOUNTAIN MYTH
Unionism in Western North Carolina

The Fifth Skull

A HISTORICAL NOVEL OF THE CIVIL WAR
AND THE AMERICAN WEST

Terrell T. Garren

THE REPRINT COMPANY, PUBLISHERS
Spartanburg, South Carolina
2008

Copyright © 2008 Terrell T. Garren
All rights reserved

An original publication, 2008
THE REPRINT COMPANY, PUBLISHERS
Spartanburg, South Carolina

ISBN 978-0-87152-561-1
Library of Congress Control Number: 2008935562
Manufactured in the United States of America

The paper used in this publication meets the minimum requirements of
American National Standard for Information Science—Permanence of Paper
for Printed Library Materials, ANSI Z39.48-1984.

MAJOR GENERAL WILLIAM NELSON, USA
1824-1862
The Union Army's "Patton"

General William Nelson

PHOTOGRAPH COURTESY OF THE MASSACHUSETTS
COMMANDERY MILITARY ORDER OF THE LOYAL LEGION
AND THE U.S. ARMY MILITARY HISTORY INSTITUTE

This work is dedicated to Major General William Nelson of Kentucky. He was a no-nonsense military leader of the highest order. He not only led his men, he fought with them. He was the Union hero at the Battle of Shiloh and was severely wounded at the Battle of Richmond, Kentucky.

Historians have often lamented the fact that the Union army didn't have a commander in the field that would have pursued Confederate

General Lee after the Union victory at Gettysburg. Had an aggressive combat leader done so, Lee's army could have been cut off before he could get back to Virginia. The bloodied Confederate commander was out of supplies, ammunition, and will. The war would have ended there and then. It was one of the greatest military mistakes in American history. A strong commander might have saved a third of a million lives and prevented untold suffering.

The Union army once had just such a commander. He was known to Lincoln and might very well have been in a position to end the war after Gettysburg. He was General William Nelson, whom I compare with our World War II hero, General George Patton. But it could not be, because Nelson was brutally murdered by an assassin, a man in his own command. The murderer was Jefferson Columbus Davis of Indiana. When one lists the most vile, evil characters of our history such as John Wilkes Booth and Lee Harvey Oswald, another name should be added: Jefferson Columbus Davis.

Contents

Preface ix
Acknowledgments xiii

PART ONE

CHAPTER 1 Waynesville, North Carolina, August 1, 1915 3
CHAPTER 2 Battlefield, Northern Virginia, April 20, 1864 13
CHAPTER 3 Edneyville, North Carolina, April 20, 1864 21
CHAPTER 4 Edneyville, North Carolina, April 28, 1864 29
CHAPTER 5 Edneyville, North Carolina, April 30, 1864 37
CHAPTER 6 Hendersonville, North Carolina, May 1, 1864 43
CHAPTER 7 Asheville, North Carolina, June 1, 1864 51
CHAPTER 8 Greeneville, Tennessee, June 1, 1864 53
CHAPTER 9 Asheville, North Carolina, June 20, 1864 57
CHAPTER 10 Greasy Cove, Tennessee, June 25, 1864 63
CHAPTER 11 Camp Vance, Morganton, North Carolina, June 28, 1864 ... 67
CHAPTER 12 Winding Stairs, North Carolina, June 29, 1864 73

PART TWO

CHAPTER 13 Cairo, Illinois, July 23, 1864 81
CHAPTER 14 Chicago, Illinois, July 24, 1864 85
CHAPTER 15 Chicago, Illinois, July 25, 1864 89

CHAPTER 16 Chicago, Illinois, August 18, 1864 95
CHAPTER 17 Chicago, Illinois, October 30, 1864 101
CHAPTER 18 Chicago, Illinois, November 15, 1864 107
CHAPTER 19 Chicago, Illinois, December 10, 1864 111
CHAPTER 20 Chicago, Illinois, December 17, 1864 113
CHAPTER 21 St. Louis, Missouri, January 23, 1864 119

PART THREE

CHAPTER 22 Fort Leavenworth, Kansas, February 12, 1865 125
CHAPTER 23 Fort Kearney, Nebraska Territory, March 10, 1865 131
CHAPTER 24 Platte River, Nebraska Territory, March 18, 1865 135
CHAPTER 25 Fort Kearney, Nebraska Territory, April 12, 1865 139
CHAPTER 26 Fort Kearney, Nebraska Territory, April 20, 1865 143
CHAPTER 27 Fort Kearney, Nebraska Territory, June 30, 1865 147
CHAPTER 28 Camp Douglas, Utah Territory, September 17, 1865 . . .151
CHAPTER 29 Fort Klamath, Oregon, November 11, 1872 155
CHAPTER 30 Yreka, California, November 15, 1872 161
CHAPTER 31 Lava Beds, Northern California, November 20, 1872 . . .169
CHAPTER 32 Portland, Oregon, November 29, 1872 175
CHAPTER 33 Lava Beds, Northern California, April 10, 1873 179
CHAPTER 34 Fort Klamath, Oregon, May 1, 1873 187
CHAPTER 35 Fort Klamath, Oregon, June 1, 1873 193
CHAPTER 36 Fort Klamath, Oregon, October 1, 1873 197
CHAPTER 37 Fort Klamath, Oregon, October 3, 1873 201
CHAPTER 38 Fort Klamath, Oregon, October 4, 1873 209
CHAPTER 39 Graham County, North Carolina, September 3, 1915 . . .219

Historical Perspective 225
About the Author 235

Preface

I would like to advise the reader that while this story is wrapped in documented history it is a work of fiction. It involves the experiences of fictional characters that are loosely based on the lives of Captain William Preston Lane, William Nicholas Clark, and J. A. Stepp, three Henderson County boys who were all caught up in some way by the Confederate Conscription Act of February 18, 1864. The Confederate government was desperate for manpower by this point in the war and the new law called all boys on their seventeenth birthday to mandatory military service.

I use the characters to take the reader through several unusual and disappointing periods in our history. The first period involves the conscription of seventeen-year-olds and their capture at Camp Vance in Morganton, North Carolina. The second period involves their experiences at the horrific Union prison at Camp Douglas in Chicago, Illinois. The third period chronicles their decision to join the Union army and their service in the "Galvanized Yankee" regiments on the western frontier. Their service in the Union army places them in northern California at the time of the bizarre Modoc Indian War.

There are plenty of stories about this period that approach the history from a traditional standpoint; my story does not. It examines the darker, more sinister side of this history. I reexamine what has been forgotten, overlooked, or covered up. Some of it is not only strange but also exposes unethical conduct on the part of some individuals in our history.

In addition to showcasing the fictional characters the story also explores the lives of many real figures from the pages of American history. Some of these faces from history were relatively minor. Some were in very high government positions. Two of the main historical figures are identified as criminals in my story: U.S. Army Colonel Jefferson Columbus Davis of Indiana, and U.S. Army Colonel Benjamin Sweet of Wisconsin. Davis was a known murderer, a charge that is not in dispute. He ambushed his own commanding officer, Major General William Nelson, in a hotel lobby and killed him in cold blood; it was a premeditated attack. Sweet was the commander of the Union Camp Douglas and was responsible for some of the worst atrocities in American history. It is the personal opinion of the author that both not only committed murder, they got away with it.

The Fifth Skull explores some of the odd occurrences during their commands. The story presents fictional representations of some theories. Some of these theories may or may not explain the seemingly insane things that happened during the Modoc War and the period immediately following. Some of the evidence regarding what really happened behind the scenes is locked away in vaults in Washington, D.C., and Suitland, Maryland, or lost forever. My representations of what happened beyond documented history are theoretical and cannot be proven. There is a lot of "smoke" but getting to the "fire" is more difficult. All of the dialogue, whether on the part of historical figures or fictional characters, is totally fictional.

Mixing fiction and documented history is a dangerous and challenging endeavor if one hopes to give an accurate representation of the period. I have done my best to present a compelling fictional story while keeping the historical representations within reasonable bounds.

Overall, the United States Army has conducted itself more humanely and decently than any other army in the history of the world. Millions of Americans have served honorably and given their lives in the U.S. Army. As a people, we can all be proud of that. But in any time of war bad people will surface and worm their way into positions of power. They always have; they always will. Sometimes war mixes evil men with power. It is valuable and important that we know about such men even if it is many years after the fact. The reader is also advised that this history exposes some very unpleasant realities. It is not appropriate reading for children.

Acknowledgments

I would like to express my deepest appreciation for my wife, Maria, and my daughter, Solari. Thank you for all your help and understanding.

I would also like to thank Reba Rattler, who helped me understand what a Snowbird Cherokee is, and Trena Parker, who helped with the original research on Colonel Gillem. I also express my sincere appreciation to Jasmine Kimmel, one of the best researchers in the state. No matter where the bones are hidden she will dig them up. I thank Jackie Smith for the cover art and helping me with the Cherokee language. In addition, I thank Susan Snowden of Snowden Editorial Services for her help in editing this work.

I also thank Dr. Richard Sommers and the staff at the U.S. Army Military History Institute. In addition I thank the staffs at Lava Beds National Monument, the Klamath Museum, the National Anthropological Archives, and the Smithsonian Institute. All have been helpful in a variety of ways.

A special thank you goes to Gale Benfield and the staff at the Burke County, North Carolina Public Library. I also want to recognize the staffs of the North Carolina Office of Archives and History, Pack Memorial Library, and the Tennessee State Archives.

The Fifth Skull

A HISTORICAL NOVEL OF THE CIVIL WAR
AND THE AMERICAN WEST

PART ONE

Chapter One

—— AUGUST 1, 1915 ——

Waynesville, North Carolina
Former Confederate Colonel William Stringfield greeted the strange visitor with courtesy, but with curiosity. It seemed to Stringfield that the man was dressed for a walk on Fifth Avenue, not a trip to the Cherokee Reservation. Stringfield's old friends in Washington, D.C., had arranged the meeting. The old Confederate colonel was to be the stranger's guide.

"Mr. Wosley, I presume," Stringfield said as he directed the dapper gentleman to the wagon.

"Yes, Colonel, I would be the same," Wosley responded politely.

Wosley climbed on the wagon and gazed into the distance. As his eyes scanned the beautiful Balsam range he took a deep breath. "My, what a splendid place. It is beautiful," he said with a warm smile and a pleasant tone. "I say, Stringfield, don't we have a long way to travel?"

"Yes, but the biggest problem is the places you want to go. We can go to Quallatown and on to Robbinsville by wagon but the roads are rough. If we get rain they'll be even worse. Sometimes you just can't go," Stringfield warned.

"Has it been dry of late, Colonel?"

"Yes, I reckon it has. Quite dry."

"Good, then we should leave today. Before it rains."

The two men stopped at the Stringfield home long enough for Wosley to change. Wosley screeched with delight upon meeting three Cherokees who waited with saddled horses to accompany the special visitor and Colonel Stringfield across the mountains.

"*Sho*, Cho-ga-See," the Indians called as the pair pulled into the yard. Cho-ga-See was the old colonel's Cherokee name. Most Cherokees were in the Confederate army during the Civil War. Stringfield was their leader in war and after the death of Colonel William Holland Thomas he became their benefactor in peace.

"*Sho, sho*," Stringfield greeted them in Kituhwa, the native Cherokee language.

Stringfield packed their supplies and checked the horses. When all was ready they began at a slow pace and headed southwest. He laughed to himself as he observed his charge's attire. He looked like a stage performer to the old colonel.

Wosley beamed with excitement as he turned to Stringfield, calling out loudly, "Cho-ga-See, onward!"

The Indians riding along behind looked at each other and chuckled. One of them gestured toward the passenger saying, "*A-da-ne-lo-hv-s-ga*," the Kituhwa word for actor. The other Indians laughed while repeating the word.

Progress was slow but the dry August weather offered better roads, along with plenty of dust. The bumpy ride was difficult for the old soldier but his visitor seemed unbothered.

They crossed Soco Gap and the Indian boundary late in the afternoon. Wosley expressed delight at being on the Indian reservation as they started down the other side of the divide. When they arrived at Quallatown darkness was nearly upon them.

Many Cherokees came out and greeted them warmly. Their relationship was such that the Cherokees often stayed, nine or ten at a time, at the

Stringfield home. It was for this reason that Wosley had chosen Stringfield to be his guide for this visit.

The pair were up before daylight having spent a night in a Cherokee lodge. Wosley explored his immediate surroundings while Cherokee women cooked bacon on an open fire. The visitor spread his arms and took a deep breath. He was obviously enjoying himself. Stringfield and the Cherokees watched him with amusement. Speaking in Kituhwa, they made fun of his dress and his new boots. Thinking him unaware they chuckled among themselves.

With an Indian escort in place the men left Quallatown and headed for Graham County and the little village of Robbinsville. The county had been formally organized in 1872, but in 1915 the town and its surroundings still seemed more like wilderness. There were few buildings to be seen. Most people still lived in cabins and there were many natives.

They rode through the town to the west passing the grave of the great Cherokee leader Junaluska, who had saved Andrew Jackson's life at the Battle of Horse Shoe Bend. Wosley insisted on stopping for a brief visit to the gravesite.

They traveled on until stopping at the home of the local Indian leader named Cornsilk.

"This is Chief Cornsilk," Stringfield said as Wosley and the Indian stared at each other.

Wosley thrust his hand forward and Cornsilk took it with some discomfort. After an exchange of greetings Conrsilk looked at Colonel Stringfield with curiosity. "Cho-ga-See, is this the man who seeks John Rattler?"

"Yes, it is. He wishes to speak to him in person."

Cornsilk looked at the dapper stranger and smiled. He turned to the Indian party escorting the group and spoke softly in Kituhwa. "He sell him Bible or whiskey, I cannot say which."

The Indians all burst out laughing and Wosley laughed with them.

They had no idea that he recognized the Kituhwa words for sell, bible, and whiskey.

Cornsilk turned back to Stringfield. "We go alone, you me, and *a-da-ne-lo-hv-s-ga*. Rattler make no room for all," he said calmly as he took charge of the group.

Wosley headed for the wagon and again the Indians laughed.

"Mr. Wosley, I'm afraid the wagon will have to stay. We'll be walking from here," Stringfield said.

"Very well then," Wosley replied. "I must get my journals."

The two men fell in behind Cornsilk and they started to hike up the narrow creek valley running between huge mountains on either side. Wosley marveled at the scenery as Stringfield reminded himself of what a beautiful place it was.

After two hours of brisk walking and crossing two sizable streams they stopped for water.

"Tell me, Cornsilk, is Rattler a Snowbird?" Wosley asked watching the old Indian's face.

Cornsilk pondered the question and nodded. "Rattler is Snowbird; he is of Snowbird spirit. He is of my people, like Little Will."

Cornsilk's answer to the question caught Stringfield's attention. He looked at the old Indian with great curiosity. He had never met John Rattler but he was puzzled by Cornsilk's words. If Rattler was a Snowbird as was Little Will, he apparently meant that Rattler was a white man. "Little Will" was the name given to the adopted white chief of the Cherokees, William Holland Thomas. He was the same man who'd formed the legion and led the Cherokees into the Confederacy and the war.

Stringfield was baffled; he was sure he would have known of such a white man. The Snowbirds were Cherokees but they considered themselves separate. He knew that they would be a lot less likely to accept a white man.

"Look, Wosley," Stringfield said. "I'm afraid you might be headed for some disappointment. You didn't take to what Cornsilk just said. But I think you may have come all this way for nothing. You wanted to see Indians and I think he just said Rattler was a white man."

"Don't be concerned, Colonel. I took what he said just as he meant it."

Stringfield was now totally bewildered by his mysterious guest. He began to realize that Wosley was not as silly and shallow as his dress seemed to indicate.

The trio hiked three more hours nonstop up Big Snowbird Creek deep into the wilderness. They hiked in silence as they took in the scenery. A golden eagle soared overhead as they made their way. Even in early August it was relatively cool along the streambed trail.

They came to a fork in the trail with a narrow path winding up into a small cove set deeper in the woods. Cornsilk pointed and led them up the path. They worked through a convoluted maze of rhododendron until they came to a small clearing of an acre or two. At the opposite side of the clearing there stood a small cabin made of hand-hewn logs and covered with a shake roof, which was partially grown over with moss. Wisps of smoke rose from a crude stone chimney where the mountain breeze tossed them about. The smell of meat cooking penetrated the air.

Cornsilk turned to the men behind him and held up his palm, indicating that they should stop where they were. Stringfield showed his exhaustion, gasping as he waved to acknowledge the signal. Wosley nodded and smiled as he watched the Indian approach the cabin.

Soon Cornsilk emerged from the cabin and signaled for the visitors to come forward. Stringfield began to get nervous as they approached the cabin. He always trusted his instincts and he was uneasy about this entire affair. His trepidation increased as they entered the cabin. At the opposite end of the structure stood a man about seventy years of age. He was dark complected and dressed as a Cherokee, but it was apparent that he was a white man, not a blood Snowbird. Beside him a woman stood slightly crouched, staring at them in silence. She was short and stocky with dark reddish skin. Her physical features were clearly native.

The strange Cherokee appeared uneasy while the visitors gawked in return.

"*Sho*," Stringfield said as he bowed toward the two strangers.

"*Sho*, Cho-ga-see," the man responded.

"*Sho, sho*," Wosley blurted out with a big smile revealing that he knew the Kituhwa word for greetings.

"Well, Wosley, I hope you know why we're here because those two aren't all that sure of us." Stringfield's voice made it clear that he was uneasy.

Wosley only smiled.

Cornsilk spoke to the light-skinned Indian in Kituhwa and the man responded in kind. While he talked his eyes studied Wosley and Stringfield with suspicion.

"He knows of you, Cho-ga-See, but has no trust for your visitor," Cornsilk said.

Before Stringfield could respond Wosley spoke over him. "John Rattler, I have come far to see you."

For a moment there was no reply. Then the man responded quietly. "Why have you come to me?" Rattler asked. "I am just a lonely Indian, living a peaceful life with my wife and my grandchildren. I have nothing to offer friend or foe."

The little Indian woman came closer to her husband and shielded half her body behind him. She peered around him as the conversation continued.

"Oh, but I think you do. I seek justice for things of the past. I think you can help me," Wosley said calmly.

John Rattler appeared mildly agitated. He stared at the visitor while sliding his right hand in the pocket of his worn leather britches. His eyes gleamed and his brow furrowed.

Stringfield intervened with a raised voice. "Hold on now, Wosley, be careful what you say. We're in another man's house."

"Who are you?" Rattler asked, his voice revealing growing anger and impatience.

"First, may I ask who are you?" Wosely said smiling.

"Now that's enough!" Stringfield interrupted, almost shouting. "I told you, we're in another man's house. You don't talk like that down here."

Wosley continued unaffected. "Did you ever serve under the command of Colonel Jefferson C. Davis of Indiana?" Wosley said, blurting out the question.

Upon hearing the name of Davis the little Indian woman began screaming at the top of her lungs. "*A-gv-ha-li-ha-ah-shko-le-a-ni-gi! A-gv-ha-li-ah-shko-le-a-ni-ga!*" she yelled as she dashed behind her husband crying and sobbing.

Rattler pulled a revolver from his pocket and pointed it at Wosley.

Cornsilk raised his hand and shouted, urging for calm.

"Don't shoot, he's crazy!" Stringfield begged as he stared at the end of the gun. "You can't kill a crazy man!"

"What is she screaming about?" Stringfield asked Cornsilk.

"She say white man came to cut off her head. Will take her head," Cornsilk answered, obviously confused.

Cornsilk turned and stared at Wosley as if he were the devil himself.

"Cut off her head? That's crazy. Why would she say something like that?" Stringfield said in utter disbelief.

Wosley didn't flinched as he stared back at John Rattler. After several uncomfortable moments he turned to the other bewildered visitors. He shook his head up and down, then looked back at the couple hovering behind the gun.

"No, no, it's not crazy at all. If you knew what they have been through." His voice seemed to convey sympathy.

"I am very sorry," he told her. "I did not mean to frighten you. I come in peace. I do not want your head. You need not fear me."

She seemed to understand his words and visibly relaxed. Rattler lowered the gun and held it by his side. Calm returned to the room as the two visitors exhaled, clearly relieved.

"For God's sake, someone tell me what the hell is going on here," Stringfield said.

"Why have you come?" Rattler asked Wosley.

"I am Arthur Limington Wosley of the *London News*. I do not seek your head, only the story trapped within it. You came here long ago hiding from something. You don't need to hide any longer. You have a chance to bring justice to this world even for those long passed."

Wosley motioned to his pocket. "I have a note for you. It's from your friend Yorkie. You do remember him, don't you?"

Rattler's eyes opened wide. He stared in disbelief. The little Indian woman peered out from behind her husband. She looked up at him, then back at the stranger.

"Yorkie?" she said quietly.

Wosley stepped forward and handed the note to Rattler. He knew Rattler was literate.

Rattler opened the folded paper and read silently. Within a few seconds tears poured from his eyes. He looked at his wife and repeated the words.

"Yorkie, it's from Yorkie." Then both of them burst into tears. Rattler held his wife in his arms as the two sobbed openly in front of the strangers.

"Will you please tell me of those times long ago? I respect the spirits." Wosley paused as he bowed his head slightly.

Rattler stood in silence for several minutes. He turned to his woman as if to ask her opinion. "I must think on it. I must talk to the spirits. You come back tomorrow and I will give you my answer," Rattler said.

———

On the following day the party returned to the cabin on Big Snowbird Creek. They sat with Rattler and the woman, sharing cornbread and slices of venison.

"I am an old man and my life will pass me soon," Rattler said. "I will join the spirits where a man is neither red nor any other color. I am tired and old and I have little reason to hide anymore. I will tell you of my life past, but I don't know where to begin."

Wosley shook his head and smiled. "Tell me from the beginning. How it all started, when you went to war, and what war did to you." Wosley took out his journal and prepared to write. Then he looked at Cornsilk and Stringfield and thanked them. "Your part in this is done. Leave us now for I shall be here for quite a while."

Wosley and the Rattlers exchanged courtesies with the two men as they departed.

The writer pulled up a chair and removed a stack of fine paper from his leather case. He lifted the ink bottle and unscrewed its top, then placed it on the crude table. After dipping his pen in the ink, he looked up at Rattler. "I know you are not John Rattler. Please state your full name."

There was little reaction at first, then Rattler responded. "You are wrong. I am John Rattler now." There was a dignified confidence to the man's words. "But not always. There was a time when I was not Cherokee; I was a white man."

Chapter Two

—— APRIL 20, 1864 ——

On the battlefield, Northern Virginia
It was an ordinary morning except for the fog. It crept along the creek banks, slowly drifting among the trees and across the fields. It slithered around and among the tents where men began to stir, like an amorphous spirit seeking but never finding a resting place.

The dashing young general rose from his cot as if he were conscious of the silent invader. He lit his lantern in the dim light of the early morning and took a deep breath. He looked toward the ground and watched the white mist that crept under the edge of his field tent. Billy Long was brave and fearless, yet he found the presence of the fog unsettling. He cast the thought aside for he knew the challenge of the day required all his attention and all the skill he could muster. Today was his day of destiny and he knew it.

Young Billy thought of his mother as he saw her image in his mind. He could visualize his older brothers, who had also fought bravely for the South. He was saddened by the mental image of his older brother standing on crutches, his left leg missing. The brave young officer tried to put it out of his mind as he began the simple routine of putting on his gray uniform.

It was new; the color was pure and the cloth crisp. The black stripes along the shoulders and down the outside of the pants legs reminded him that it was a North Carolina uniform, something he was proud of. He slipped on the pants, then slid on his boots with little effort.

"General Long," he said aloud as he looked at himself in the tiny field mirror.

So many men looked up to him now, he must do his duty. He would face death today, yet he was not afraid. Leading men was his destiny and he would not falter. He would do as others had done before him and if it cost him life or limb it would be God's will.

The youthful officer splashed cool water on his face yet he didn't seem to feel it. His mind drifted to and fro, from home and family to his men and the pending battle. He thought of General Lee and was inspired by his vision.

"I will not disappoint you, sir," he said aloud. "I will do as you ordered, I will take that hill."

He envisioned his father and remembered his admonition, "Make us proud, son."

Young Billy saw his mother crying but he could not comfort her for she didn't understand. This was man's work. He forced himself to put the troubling image out of his mind. General Long pulled the gray tunic over his shoulders and buttoned the double-breasted front quickly.

He put on his hat and belted on his straight-bladed infantry officer's sword. Holding the tiny mirror in his hand he scanned himself, admiring the beautiful uniform.

"If I die today I shall be properly dressed to meet my maker," he thought.

He took a deep breath and reached for his Colt revolver and slowly slipped it into the holster opposite his sword. He patted the handle and thought of it as a reliable friend.

Taking another breath he remembered the words of General Lee, "Keep the sun to your back, young man, keep the sun to your back."

Fear skipped through his mind as he stepped toward the flaps at the end of his tent but he cast it aside. He bent and flipped the tent flap open and stepped outside. A large fire burned at the center of many tents. Dozens of officers were gathered around warming their hands and looking into the fire. The eerie fog drifted around their legs and among the tents.

The young general stood erect and walked toward the fire. All the others turned to witness his confident approach. They stood at attention and greeted their brigade commander with reverence and respect.

"Would you like to eat, sir?" one man asked.

Long looked at him as if he were deranged. "No, there is not time," he responded. "Bring me my horse."

He stared at the men in front of him with adrenalin beginning to flow through his veins. His heart beat a little faster and his breathing picked up speed.

Beyond the fire he saw an old soldier walking his beautiful black stallion toward the encampment. The horse was large and shining with saddle in place. Long walked toward the group of men as they slowly parted to give him passage. All eyes were on him as he approached the stallion. The old soldier held the horse as the general mounted. Once in the saddle he looked down at the old man and thanked him.

The white-bearded veteran looked up at him and whispered as if to convey a secret. "Remember what General Lee told you, keep the sun to your back."

Long looked at the cluster of officers gathered around the fire. They stood motionless and stared back at him. "Gentlemen, form your regiments," he shouted.

Suddenly the cluster of men began to scramble in all directions, running to and fro. Long could hear their unorganized chatter as they shouted or mouthed, "Yes, sir. Yes, sir."

The dashing figure on the horse was amused but untroubled. He knew his men and he understood that they would follow him to the death. He could hear the rustle and the shouts going up and down the line.

"Fall in, men. Form your ranks," he could hear them shout. Regimental commanders shouted to the company commanders and the company captains shouted to the soldiers. Men poured from among the trees and from behind the rocks. At first there were hundreds and then there were thousands. Within minutes his brigade stood in perfect formation ready for battle. There were six regiments of North Carolina men totaling over seven thousand waiting for his command.

Billy Long sat motionless in the saddle and watched his men form. It was an amazing sight and he swelled with pride as he watched. "Bring up the color guard," he shouted with all his might.

Hearing another officer repeat his order he turned to see a smaller cluster of men coming out of the trees and unfurling the flags. The mounted young general looked down the line and saw the regimental color guards repeating the same pre-battle ritual. Soon Confederate battle flags were flapping in the wind in front of all six regiments.

Long turned toward the brigade color bearers and shouted, "Form the brigade colors, front and center."

Immediately the men rushed down the line and into formation in front of the regiments. Turning to the right and facing the hill, they formed perfectly in the center. When all were in place Brigadier General William Nicholas Long nudged his black stallion into a gentle canter. He rode all the way down the line waving his hat. The men of his Confederate brigade broke into a roaring cheer. His horse seemed to float along as thousands of men removed their hats and waved in a jubilant response. He continued his ride feeling no bumps or bounce from the impact of the horse's hooves. After passing the last regiment he reared his horse, turned, and rode back to the center where the brigade colors were assembled. He reined in his horse facing his men with his back to the hill and the enemy.

He stared past his men, over them, and to the woods beyond. He watched the rising sun as it stirred behind the sea of Confederate gray. The morning light was held at bay by the woods and the low ridge in the distance. Long watched and waited as the sun came up slowly behind the trees. At first the light only leaked through the limbs and the branches. Within a few minutes the light peeked over the trees and brightened the sky.

The dashing young general turned and faced the enemy. As the sun rose, it cast a brilliant gold light onto the hill beyond. Even though he was several hundred yards away he could see figures in blue scurrying about. He could not hear them but he could see officers pointing at him and frantically waving their hands.

The young commander detected a presence at his side. He turned and looked into the eyes of the old soldier who'd fetched his horse.

"Look, General," the old man said. "The fog is gone; it is your time."

"Yes," Long replied. "It is time."

The young commander dismounted, handed the reins to the old man, and drew his sword. Then, with all the power God gave his voice, he shouted, "Forwaaard. Forwaaard!" His voice boomed over the field with supernatural effect.

Regimental commanders turned to their regiments and repeated the order with equal volume. "Forrrwaaard!" they screamed up and down the line.

The company commanders followed with the same cry. "Forrrwaaard!" The words seemed to drag from their throats as the sound echoed across the field.

In unison, the whole army began to march forward to the ominous hill and the blue sea atop the formidable mound. General Long held his sword in the air as he marched in front of the brigade colors. He listened to the steady thump of thousands of feet marching behind him. He looked at the hill and smiled as he saw the sun beaming onto the blue soldiers as he led his attack.

More soldiers in blue came into view, pulling up cannons and turning their horses. He could see them holding their hands in front of their eyes struggling to see the approaching Confederates. As his men got closer and closer he watched the unorganized enemy running toward their barricades and placing their weapons.

Soon the enemy artillery began to fire but their aim was into the blinding sun and ineffective. Many shells tore into the ground and still more burst in midair. He was very close now. Adrenaline surged through his veins as he led the advance.

He lowered his sword left, then swung over and back to the right. This was the signal for the front ranks to fire. Soon company commanders moved to the left and the men in front lowered their Enfield rifles as they continued their steady march. When all was clear the captains shouted the order: "Fire!"

Bursts of smoke poured from the ends of hundreds of rifles. Bullets flew and tore into the ranks of the men in blue atop the hill. Up and down the line the company commanders repeated the order. More shots fired and more men died.

Long could see an officer on the hill garbed in full-dress uniform, double-breasted with gold buttons and gold stripes across the chest. He wore a large blue hat with gold tassels. The man raised his sword and dropped it in a signaling motion. Upon his signal the men in blue opened fire.

Long heard the lead bullets whizzing past his head. He heard men behind him cry out as the merciless fire raining from the hill struck them down. He watched the man giving the orders and recognized that he was a high-ranking general. Long pulled his revolver and fired at the man, who was now quite close to him. He tried to see his face but the enemy leader turned to the side and he could not see beyond the brim of the man's hat.

The Confederate commander shouted to his officers and twirled his sword in a circular motion. "Charge!" he yelled with all his strength.

He could barely hear the order being repeated behind him but within seconds he knew his men were following his command. Rebel yells flew up all along the battlefront as thousands of Confederates charged in unison. Soon his men were beside him and surging beyond him. The young general ran forward with his color guard waving the colors in defiant glory directly behind him.

He could hear men yelling and screaming as the frenzy of battle exploded all around him. Cannon shell burst in the air as muskets flared at close range. The smoke was so thick he could not see. The Confederate officer waved his hands in an attempt to part the smoke. He saw flashes of both blue and gray dancing through his head but could not find his way.

Concentrating with all his will he searched through the blinding smoke looking for the enemy leader. He stumbled in confusion and fired his pistol blindly. He heard men scream and he knew men were dying all around him. He dropped his pistol as the din of battle deafened him. He ripped his sword from its scabbard and thrashed blindly, not seeing or hearing.

The young general was now consumed by panic. Where is he? Long thought to himself. "If I don't find him, he'll kill me," he mumbled aloud.

Suddenly he was grabbed by the shoulder and forcibly turned around. He dropped his sword in panic and stared at the man who held him. The man grabbed him by both shoulders and shook him. Long tried to see his face but could not make it out, as the sun shone into his face and blinded him.

"Oh, God! Oh, God!" he tried to shout but no words would come. "Oh, God! The sun is in my face."

The man in the blue general's uniform continued to shake him and threw him to the ground. He climbed over the young Confederate's body and shook him hard.

Long looked up at him in total confusion. Straddling his body was the old man who'd fetched his horse. Now the old man wore the blue of a Yankee general.

The old man gritted has teeth and shouted angrily at the vanquished Confederate. "I told you to keep the sun at your back." The old man shook him more violently.

Long tried to respond but the words would not come out. He tried again. "I'm sorry. I'm so sorry," he mumbled over and over.

The old man continued to shake him as he fought for words. Then he heard the old man's voice change. "Sorry for what?" he asked.

Slowly Long's vision cleared and his senses returned.

"Git your ass out of bed," his younger brother said. "You're sorry all right. 'Bout the sorriest thing I ever saw. Come on, git up. It's your birthday, in case ya don't know, and Momma is makin' apple pie."

Billy Long sat up and scratched his eyes. "I reckon I was dreamin' 'bout the war."

"Well, they ain't no war here 'cept the chores we got," John replied without sympathy. "What's it like bein' seventeen? Do you feel older?" He laughed.

"Naw, feels just like sixteen, far as I kin tell. 'Cept one thing; I'll be old enough for the army soon."

Chapter Three

—— APRIL 20, 1864 ——

Edneyville, North Carolina
The air was scented with burning locust wood as young Billy sat up and stretched his arms. The dream lingered in his mind but he thought little of it within just a few minutes. His immediate attention was directed to the daily chores that lay ahead.

"We've got more plowin' today," he said to his little brother in a sleepy tone.

The Longs were fortunate compared to others in the area. There were two adolescent boys and three girls still at home to work the farm. The two oldest boys were in the Confederate army. James was in the Sixtieth North Carolina Infantry Regiment and Marcus was a prisoner of war being held in the Union prison at Camp Douglas in Chicago, Illinois. He was a member of the Sixty-fourth North Carolina Infantry Regiment when the entire regiment, except for those on detachment duty, was captured at Cumberland Gap, Tennessee, in September 1863. There had been no communication from him since his capture. The last word from James was that his regiment had been driven from Chattanooga and Lookout Mountain along with the rest of the Confederate Army of

Tennessee. He and the main body of the battered army were now in a defensive position at Dalton, Georgia.

The focus of everyday life for the families of Henderson County, North Carolina, was their immediate survival and news of the war. There was always a constant stream of rumors about the war—some good, some bad. Most people had learned not to pay much attention until there was some kind of confirmation or official word. Very often the official announcements turned out to be inaccurate.

Western North Carolina families had supported the Confederate effort with as much enthusiasm and spirit as any other place in the South in the beginning. But now, after three hard years of war and many horrific battles, attitudes were changing. Many held out hope for the fledgling nation but many others had growing doubts. The mountains were full of deserters and some men had gone to the other side, where shoes, food, and pay were realities. The Confederate conscription acts and the desperate fight for survival on the home front had converted some former Confederates into disgruntled doubters or outright opponents.

Young Billy and his brother, thirteen-year-old John, still held to their Confederate teachings. Billy's father, William Long, was hopeful and remained a believer. His mother, Elizabeth, hated the war, the Confederacy, the Union, and anything else that had any association with it. She wanted the war stopped and stopped now. She kept herself constantly at work to occupy her mind. She made every effort to limit any idle time, which might lead to thoughts of the war. Billy knew his mother worried constantly about her two sons in the Confederate army and she fumed at the rumors of more conscription. He had heard her vow to kill anyone who tried to take her younger sons when they came of age.

Elizabeth Long had risen early on her son's birthday to make him an apple pie. It wouldn't be a fresh pie, the kind she'd make in late summer or fall, but her own special honey apple pie.

The boys watched as Elizabeth soaked dried apples in water while she rolled thin strips of dough. She rolled longer pieces and laid them across the bottom of the black iron skillet. With practiced hands she took the shorter pieces and pressed them to the edges of the skillet. When the bottom was fully coated with strips of dough she reached into the bucket and pulled out a handful of the softened dried apple cuttings and layered them over the dough.

Next she lifted the clay-fired pot of honey saved from the previous fall. She pulled a portion of the precious substance from the container with a wooden spoon. The honey was thick and much drier than it was when William had harvested it. Elizabeth moved the spoon slowly over the apple layer while watching the honey spread at a snail's pace. When the bottom layer was complete she repeated the process placing two more layers adding small pieces of butter under the last layer. The old mountain recipe for honey apple pie required several hours of sitting while the honey soaked into the apples and the dough. She covered the black skillet with a heavy iron lid and placed it on an oak table beside the fire.

Billy's mother was Elizabeth Sanford Long. She was born in South Carolina but had moved to Henderson County as a child with her family. She married William Long while the rest of her family had moved on west. She was a Long now, through and through. Her husband and her seven children were her life and her spirit.

The Long matriarch was a petite woman, fifty-two years old. Bearing seven children, the hard farm life, and the strain of war had given her the look of a much older woman. Her once dark brown hair was streaked with gray and it hung in strings tied behind her bonnet. Her everyday work dress was all she had. Her once bright brown eyes squinted and strained as her sight faded.

Billy's father, William Long, was fifty-five, a tall man—a full six feet. He held his head high and carried his pride on his face. He was proud of his family and spoke with confidence about the war. "The Confederacy will prevail," he'd say whenever the topic arose.

Now bald he wore his floppy hat on all occasions, at work or at rest. On his farm there was not much rest. William always rousted Billy early and worked him late. He pushed his other children to do the same and for the most part they got by.

The three girls had come in order behind the older boys. Martha was the oldest of the girls, now twenty-four but unmarried. Malinda was twenty-two and Caroline nineteen. None of the girls was married, nor did they have any prospects for marriage. There were no young men of their age left in the community. They were all either in the army, physically maimed, or dead. Western North Carolina families could now count over six thousand young lives lost to the war and thousands more wounded or captured, with no end in sight.

John was the youngest and the liveliest. He found fun in everything no matter how tough the times. He was small for his age but well built and athletic. Billy marveled at his energy and complained at his constant urgings for work or play.

Billy was the tallest of the boys even at seventeen years of age. He was already six feet tall and stronger than most. He could run like the wind and follow a plow horse for hours. His sandy brown hair was lighter than that of his siblings and his eyes were hazel like his father's. Billy was square jawed but pleasant to the eye.

Young Billy was not a natural worker like his brother but he got it done. All in all, he figured they had it pretty good. The family owned a plow horse and two milk cows. They had milk and sometimes butter to sell at Edney's store. As far as they knew his two older brothers were still alive and they hoped for the best. Deep down he knew that if the war kept on he'd be called but he didn't think of it much. It was something that didn't seem real to him as he carried on his daily chores. When he turned eighteen he'd have to go but that was still a long way off. There were rumors that they would change the law and call seventeen-year-olds soon, but his father assured him that it wasn't true.

Billy and John worked the pastures while the girls milked the cows and placed corn seeds in the furrows the boys had plowed. They had no slaves so the work was their own. Billy walked a steady pace behind the old plow horse while John cleared in front of his path. Billy would sight the old horse using the top of Bearwallow Mountain in the distance as a guide. He'd plow the row, turn the horse, and steer a straight line in the other direction. He and John kept up a constant chatter as their work progressed.

The father of all these workers watched the weather and worried about rain; either too much or too little was the rule. It never seemed to be just right.

As the evening sun drifted toward the ridges the boys took the plow horse to the barn and unhitched the harness. The girls went to the well and washed the mud and dirt from their bare feet and fingers. William and Billy had crude and well-worn leather shoes but the women and John worked in bare feet.

That night the family gathered around the large hand-hewn table in the center of the main room of the old log house. The smell of chestnut logs and an open fire drifted around the room. They said a prayer and asked the Lord to watch over James and Marcus. The family patriarch added a few words for a Confederate victory, then they all focused on the sparse but adequate meal prepared by Elizabeth. There was a pot full of early greens with corn bread and slices of bacon. The girls broke their cornbread into bowls of milk while the two boys ate theirs separately.

Billy watched his father as he looked over the table and smiled. For all their troubles they were still happy. If only the war would end, they could all be together again.

At last it was time for the pie. Elizabeth pulled the big black skillet off the fire and placed it in the center of the table. Billy Nick, as they often called him, was to get the first piece. It was his birthday and the honey apple pie was his favorite dish. Unlike the others he seemed to like it better than the traditional pie made from fresh in-season apples.

His father scooped out a large portion and dropped it on Billy's tin plate. Billy took his spoon and tore into it with little fanfare or manners.

"Well, happy birthday, son," his mother said laughing at his antics.

"Happy birthday," was the call around the table as they all waited their turn for the precious treat.

"It's a good thing ya made a big un, Maw, else I wouldn't git none," John wailed as he watched his brother gobble the pie.

As the evening wore on the family laughed and played, truly enjoying young Billy Nick's birthday. The worries of war and the future were absent if for only a flash in time. Elizabeth enjoyed herself more than usual but still not as much as the others. Trepidation at some level was always there even in the best of times. She watched them all and thanked God for what little she did have.

Late in the evening John stoked the fire as Billy Nick went for more firewood. Late April in southern Appalachia brought warmer days but the days were often followed by nights with a biting chill. A steady wind from the north would make a fire necessary throughout the night. After rebuilding the fire, John and Billy returned to the little attachment of a room where they slept. The girls giggled and talked as they climbed to the loft where they all slept together in one makeshift feather bed.

Billy buried himself in the warm quilts his mother had made.

"Boy, that pie was a good un," John whispered as he lay his head on the soft down pillow.

"Best I ever had," Billy responded. "Reckon it's all gone though."

"I wish I was seventeen like you, all growed up," John commented.

"I reckon it's all right; don't seem much different to me though," Billy answered.

"Do ya think you'll have to go to the army next year?"

"Naw, I don't think so. Paw says the war'll be over by then."

John drifted off to sleep and Billy thought about his brothers. He and his mother worried the most about Marcus because he was a prisoner. Returning Confederate soldiers told horrible stories about the Union prisons. Many had been exchanged and sent back south. The new Union commander, someone named Grant, had stopped the exchanges knowing that the Confederates couldn't replace their men and the Union army could. Still, Billy prayed every day for reinstatement of the exchange program or an end to the war.

As he lay there, Billy Nick remembered the strange dream. His memory of it was haunting. He wondered what it was like being in the army, in the war, or worse, in a prison. "Thank God I don't have to worry about that," he said to himself as he closed his eyes and drifted off.

Chapter Four

—— APRIL 28, 1864 ——

Edneyville, North Carolina
The morning sun barely penetrated the cold morning air as William Long wrestled the stiff leather harness onto the horse's body. Breath from both horse and man was visible as they shivered from the cold.

"Atta girl," he said as he led the horse from the barn.

He guided her to the wagon where Billy waited. After positioning the animal the two hitched the horse to the small wagon the family used to carry both man and supplies. It was so small it couldn't carry much, but that was just as well because the horse couldn't pull much.

William Long tied the horse to a dogwood tree and the two went into the house to warm themselves. Standing in front of the fire they turned to and fro as they attempted to absorb the heat. The elder Long turned his back to the smoking embers as he addressed his wife. "Maw, me 'n' Billy are goin' down to Edney's store. We need more seed."

"Don't be gone too long and y'all keep warm. It's colder 'n jack frost out there."

The two Longs left the house and started down the road toward Balis Edney's store. It was the only place within miles to get seed and other supplies needed by area farmers. Billy walked alongside the wagon to lighten the horse's load and William sat on the wagon seat as he urged the horse forward.

"Paw, you reckon Edney has any salt yet?" the youngster asked as he strolled along the edge of the slightly muddy road.

"I don't know, boy, but we're needin' it somethin' awful," his father replied. "He ain't had none for weeks now. Says he can't git none."

"If we git half that hog the Freemans promised, we're gonna have to have salt," Billy said.

"I know, boy, ya can't keep meat if ya can't preserve it."

"I'd give anything for a belly full of fresh pork right now," Billy said wistfully.

"Me too, boy, but right now we best git the rest of our corn in the ground."

The old plow horse plodded along as Billy looked around at the budding spring that surrounded them. He noticed the early dogwoods and the spring frost on the greening grass. As the sun climbed higher in the brilliant blue sky the day seemed to portend a brighter future.

The sound of the squeaky wagon wheels shrieked across the valley as the horse's hooves clomped along. Soon the old wagon crested the hill and the store came into view. There were many wagons gathered around and clusters of people milled about in the yard.

"Look, Paw, it's busier 'n bees down there. I bet he's got salt."

The older man took his eyes off the road long enough to look off down the valley. "I hope it is salt. That'd be a good present for us all."

As they made their way down the road Billy could see that the sight became more and more disconcerting to the elder Long. They had seen this kind of thing before and it wasn't usually a good thing.

Billy looked at the moving crowd with some excitement. "Sure is a lot of folks down there." He wondered what the news might be. Very often this kind of gathering meant reports of a battle, casualty lists, or some other news of the war. It was the spring of 1864 and the winter had been relatively quiet. Maybe peace was at hand.

They pulled up the wagon some distance from the store where there was room to stop. William jumped off and spoke gruffly to his son. "You stay with the wagon, Billy. I'm goin' in to see what all the fuss is about."

"Let's tie up the horse. I wanna go too," Billy shouted.

"No," the older man snapped back.

Deep down they both knew that a casualty list might contain the name of one of the Long boys. William Long didn't want Billy to see until he knew what the news was. "No, you stay here. All these damn people might spook her. I'll be right back, son," he instructed with a calmer voice.

Long turned and started for the store. There were several veterans standing around, one with a missing arm; another with only one leg stood with the help of a crutch. Long could hear the rumblings of mixed conversations.

Old Hiram Lamb recognized him as he approached the porch and addressed him by his childhood nickname.

"Hey, Willie, don't you fret none. This war's gonna be over soon."

Long's fear surged as he wondered why Lamb said that to him.

"Oh, God, don't let it be my boys," he said to himself as he climbed the stairs at the end of the loading dock. "Please, God." He thought briefly of Elizabeth and couldn't bear to think of how she'd react.

He had to work his way through people to reach the open door to the store.

Balis Edney was not only the owner of the store he was also the highest ranking Confederate in Henderson County. He'd been given a captain's rank at the beginning of the war and he'd formed a company right here in Edneyville; however, difficult duties and a dispute with his commanding officer, Colonel Thomas Clingman, had resulted in Edney's resignation and his return to Henderson County.

Once at home Edney became a colonel in the North Carolina Militia, which became the Home Defense Forces after the passage of the Confederate Conscription Act of July 1863. Edney was an educated man who'd been United States ambassador to Sicily before the war. He was also a lawyer. Now he was in charge of enforcing Confederate conscription among a population whose tolerance for it was waning every day. His current duty was among his toughest yet.

Long saw Edney at the back of the store seated with Lieutenant Gideon Orr and Sergeant Julius Whitaker. Whitaker often acted as Edney's assistant. Orr was in charge of the men of the Forty-first Battalion of the Confederate Militia. The short nickname for these men was "home guard." The two of them sat leaning over a small table and seemed to be going over a list while several local men watched.

As Long worked his way toward the back of the store he began to shake. He was a loyal Confederate but he couldn't bear the thought of losing one of his sons. As he passed through the mix of people Harmon Stepp walked away from the table and looked up at Long. He shook his head from side to side in apparent disgust. "This ain't right, Willie, it just ain't right."

"What ain't right, damn it? What the hell is goin' on?" Long raised his voice in frustration.

Stepp stopped and looked him in the eyes. He started to speak but his lips began to quiver and the old man lost his speech. Tears came to his eyes and he brushed past Long and moved on through the crowd toward the door.

Long approached the table as Edney and Whitaker looked up at him. "Good mornin' to ya, Willie," Whitaker said quietly.

"Balis, what the hell is goin' on here?" Long demanded as he lost all his patience.

Balis Edney shook his head in apparent resignation. "Thank you for coming in, William. We were coming to see you anyway. Now we won't have to."

CHAPTER FOUR

"Are ya gonna tell me what's goin' on here or not?" Long began to shake harder as his panic overtook him. He could hardly get the words out.

"Here, William. Read this," Edney said as he passed him a large sheet of paper with fancy script at the top.

"Oh, God, it's a casualty list," Long thought. "I've lost one of my boys." He began to tear up.

Long was literate but his eyesight was not so good. He looked at the heading on the paper and read the large print at the top: IN CONGRESS, CONFEDERATE STATES OF AMERICA.

"I can't see the rest of it, what does this mean?" Long asked almost pleading.

Edney looked up at him with resignation on his face. "It's a change in the conscription law. They've created something called the Junior Reserve. They're calling all seventeen-year-olds to the army on their birthday. There's no choice, William, we just don't have enough men."

William Long stood totally shocked; his mouth fell open and his eyes widened. "Oh, God, no. His momma will die. She won't stand for it. Oh please no," Long said almost begging.

"You know I can't do nothin', William. It's the law," Edney said firmly. "Besides, these boys aren't going to be sent to the front. They'll do post duty at home; they'll be in Asheville or Morganton or somewhere here in North Carolina.

"I can promise you that he'll never leave North Carolina," Edney stated with confidence. "It's so the men currently doing those jobs can go to the front. The boys will have to work but they won't do any fighting."

William Long's eyes watered but he didn't cry. He hadn't cried since he was a boy and he knew he would have to be strong now. His mind whirled with confused thoughts. What could he say? What could he do? What would he say to Elizabeth?

"How do ya know they won't be fightin'? Who's to say they won't change that too?" Long almost shouted and his voice cracked with emotion.

"They just won't, William. After all, they're just boys. We know that. We've got to have the manpower. You want us to win this war, don't you?" Edney asked appealing to Long's sense of patriotism.

"When does he have to go?" Long asked regaining some of his composure.

"We'll be by to fetch him come Saturday," Sergeant Whitaker responded.

"Saturday?" Long screeched. "My God, that's just two days!"

"I'm sorry, William. We have no choice, it's the law," Edney said. "Will you bring him in Saturday so we don't have to come get him?"

Long thought of saying no, but he knew there was no option.

"Yeah, I reckon so; least his Maw won't have to see it," he said.

William Long shook terribly as he walked back through the store. He was so stunned he didn't hear the conversation or the condolences from the others in the room. He made his way to the porch where he found Harmon Stepp broken down, crying openly.

Long was moved as he put his hands on his shoulder.

Stepp looked up at him with tears flowing. "He's my last one. They've taken all my boys. Francis and Columbus are dead and we ain't heard from Robert in over a year." He barely finished his words before sobbing again.

It was all Long could do to control himself but he held on. There was no choice. He'd have to be strong. He thought of taking his family and leaving but where would they go? How would they eat? Besides, he was a committed Confederate and they had to win the war. He thought of what might happen to his daughters if the South lost the war.

He felt a tap on his shoulder and turned to see Emma Freeman, who worked in the store. She held a sack in her hand. She thrust it forward indicating he should accept it.

"It's the seed you wanted. Mr. Edney says he'll put it on the books; you don't have to pay nothin' now.

Long accepted the seed, then looked out toward the wagon and his heart raced. He could see Billy Nick craning his neck trying to figure out what was happening.

Just then, J. A. Stepp ran to the wagon, shouting the news. "Hey, Billy, have ya heard? We're goin' to the army now! Ain't that great? Whoo wee! We'll be going together!"

"What do ya mean?" Billy asked.

"They're takin' seventeen-year-olds. We're goin' Saturday."

The elder Long made his way back to the wagon and threw the sack full of corn seed in the back and climbed on. He looked at Billy with a grave expression on his face.

"I know what you're thinkin', Paw. It's alright, I'll be fine," Billy said softly.

William Long bit his lip, trying to control himself. He'd seen two of his sons off to war and now they were taking Billy Nick. He wanted to do something, to say something, but he couldn't. Finally after a long silence he shouted at the boy without looking at him. "Climb on here, son. We've gotta think."

Billy Nick climbed onto the wagon and they made a circle in the yard and headed back down the road toward home. The elder Long drove very slowly, while he tried to compose himself. Neither man said a word for over a half hour. William thought of the war, James and Marcus, and how the South needed the manpower. He considered Edney's words and wondered if it were true that the boys would do no fighting. The boy was already a good shot, just like everyone else who grew up in the mountains. But, William thought, shootin' rabbits and turkeys is a sight different than shootin' men. Especially when the men are shootin' back.

The elder Long pulled the wagon over to the side where a wide place in the road made it easier. He turned to his son and put his hand on his shoulder. "Son, if you say ya don't wanna go, they'll come huntin' ya."

Billy held his head down then looked up slowly. "I ain't afraid, Paw, I'll go."

The older man lost his composure again and could not speak. Finally the words came to him as he looked off in the trees. "I'm mighty proud of ya, boy, mighty proud," he said, but he was unable to look him in the face. "We can't tell your Maw now. I'll have to tell her after you're gone."

His father turned away as tears slipped out of the corners of Billy's eyes. The elder Long knew Billy was thinking of his mother. They both knew how upset she'd be.

"I understand, Paw, I won't tell nobody."

William Long slapped his son twice on the shoulder, then popped the reins and started the old plow horse toward home. There was no more talk between father and son. William recognized that the boy beside him was now a man.

Chapter Five

—— APRIL 30, 1864 ——

Edneyville, North Carolina
The hours flew by as father and son held their secret. The distance between farms and the constancy of the spring workload kept Elizabeth from hearing the news. She noticed their quiet demeanor but didn't make sense out of it. She was unaware of the missing blanket and the supplies that had been stored in the barn.

It was a bright spring morning and the sky was dotted with small puffy clouds. Plumes of white mist circled up from the coves like smoke from little campfires. The mountain foliage was sprouting green, and it was much warmer than it had been.

William and Billy were at the business of harnessing the horse and hitching her to the wagon. The elder Long fidgeted and worked nervously as he dreaded Elizabeth's reaction when he returned from the store without Billy. He recognized full well that she would be out of control. All his love would be needed to comfort her, to give her strength.

He thanked God for the warm weather. William hoped that the war would end before the next winter. Like everyone else he'd learned that disease was just as likely to kill his son as any battle. But he was a hardy boy, strong of mind and body.

Still, the elder Long was overcome with sadness. He looked toward the house and nearly cried as he considered that Billy's mother might never see him again. Unlike the early days of the war when jubilation and excitement overcame logic, mountain folks now knew that the hardships of war were very real.

Long sent his son to the barn to fetch his bedroll when the sound of horses and men came bounding over the hill above the house. Long turned to see who was coming. As he peered into the distance he was puzzled. Why such an assembly? he wondered. There were eight men on horseback who appeared to be headed for his farm.

The men rode into the yard and up to Long. The leader took off his hat and smiled at William. "Sergeant Julius B. Whitaker at your service, sir," he said as he swept the hat back to his head.

"What in the hell are ya doin' here? I told Balis I'd bring the boy in," Long shouted.

"No offense intended, sir. We was comin' this way anyhow. We figured to just pick the boy up as we went."

There was concern among Confederate authorities that some of the boys might run off to the mountains and hide with other relatives who'd already deserted. Their plan was to come and take the boys in order to make sure they didn't lose any.

"Damn it, Whit, we was just fixin' to come down to the store now."

As the two men argued a large freight wagon came rolling over the hill. As their discussion continued the wagon pulled up to the house. There were five seventeen-year-old boys sitting in the back including James A. Stepp, the last of the Stepp boys.

Long looked at the sight and decided it was the most pitiful thing he'd ever seen. "This here's madness and God will smite ya for it some day."

Whitaker bowed his head in recognition of the tragic situation. He'd done this kind of duty too long and he was no longer proud of his role. "Willie, this whole damned war is madness. Don't ya know I know that? Ain't nothin' I kin do 'bout it. I just gotta go on, day by day," he said with apparent sincerity. "I just got my orders from Mr. Edney. He said to come git these boys."

The sound of the barn door screeching as it opened interrupted the men's conversation. The two turned to look as Billy Nick Long walked through the barn door toward the group of men on horseback. He had his blanket rolled and tied around his back. He carried his father's small leather bag with biscuits and other supplies packed in it. There was no expression on his face as he approached the men. The youthful man walked toward them as if he were headed to plow the next row. His demeanor was calm and he held his head high.

Whitaker watched his approach with genuine appreciation. He was thankful that there'd be no trouble. He'd dealt with some of that earlier in the morning.

As Billy approached the group the front door to the house opened and Elizabeth Long came into the yard. She wore an apron and carried a large wooden spoon. "William, what's all this about?" she asked, a worried look on her face.

At first she thought of bad news about James or Marcus. Then she caught the movement coming from her left. She turned and considered the sight but could not believe her eyes. Once she saw the bedroll around her son's back the picture was clear.

Her weathered face twisted in anguish. She screamed an inaudible curse and raced to her son. Elizabeth hooked her left arm around Billy's arm and pulled him violently to her side. She pointed at Whitaker and screamed, *"I'll kill you! God curse your soul! Git off my land; you're nothin' but the devil!"*

She kept her finger pointed at Whitaker as if it were a weapon while she began to drag her son toward the house. Young Billy was torn by emotion and confusion.

"Maw, please…I gotta go," he pleaded.

"Now, 'Lizabeth, you listen here," William Long said as he moved toward her.

"No, you listen, Willie Long. I'll kill you too. You get out of my sight. You're nothin' but a traitor to your own kin." As she railed at him she began sobbing.

Billy was now crying too as he begged his mother to let him go. The other children having heard the commotion came running to the front of the house. Now all of them stood crying.

Little John mumbled through his tears but no one could hear him. "Please don't take Billy."

William Long mustered all his courage and ran to the struggling pair. He took hold of her right arm and tried to calm her. She broke her hand free and lashed at him with her nails. She scratched his face as she wailed.

Whitaker and his men sat in their saddles wide-eyed. Whitaker tried to talk but he wasn't heard. The scene was so disturbing that some of the boys on the wagon were also crying.

She turned loose of Billy long enough to swing around and strike her husband with a strong blow to the temple. Long reeled at the force of it but when she swung the second time he caught her other arm and held it tightly.

As Elizabeth screamed and struggled the other men sat speechless.

Billy looked at his mother and begged her to stop. "Please, Maw, please," he muttered through his tears.

William Long looked at Billy and nodded toward the wagon. His voice choked but he managed to get the words out. "Now go, boy, git on that wagon," he shouted as held back his own tears. He turned toward Whitaker as he watched his son move toward the wagon. "Damn it, I told ya I'd bring him in! Why didn't ya listen? If anything happens to my boy, you tell Balis I'm gonna kill him, and after I'm done I'm gonna kill you too."

"Look, Willie, I didn't start this damn war. I'm just doin' what I gotta do," Whitaker said. Whitaker looked at Elizabeth, trapped in her husband's firm grasp. "Ma'am, I'm mighty sorry. I'm doin' the best I can." His voice cracked as he uttered his feeble apology.

CHAPTER FIVE

Billy climbed onto the wagon as the other men moved out of the yard turning their horses toward Hendersonville. He watched his mother through his tears as the wagon driver whipped the reins and they pulled away.

Elizabeth Long continued to struggle and scream. Her threats were still coming as the wagon climbed the hill headed toward town. "I curse you, Julius Whitaker! May God strike ya dead for what ya done."

He didn't look back but Whitaker heard her oath as it echoed through the valley. As the wagon topped the hill Billy looked back at the farm, then higher in the sky toward Bearwallow Mountain. He caught one last glimpse of his mother and wondered to himself if he'd ever see her again again. Then he buried his face in his hands and sobbed quietly.

Chapter Six

—— MAY 1, 1864 ——

Hendersonville, North Carolina
The boys were all up early, anxious to learn what they would be doing or where they would be going. The trauma of the previous day was still fresh on their minds but their immediate concerns put those worries partially behind them. They made their camp at the town post office sleeping in the small stable behind the crude facility. The ground was hard but at least it was dry.

The town jailer brought them cold grits and hard biscuits for breakfast. Three other boys had been brought in from other parts of the county so now there were nine.

The group of soldiers-to-be sat around in clusters as they ate their breakfast. All of them had food from home, which was far better than the jail food they'd been offered by their keepers.

"Ain't this a sight? We ain't been in the army but one day 'n' they're already feedin' us jail food," Young Preston Lane complained with a laugh.

All the boys knew each other more or less. The familiarity and the commonality of their plight made them immediate comrades.

"Hear tell from my brother's letters that this jail food we're getting is a sight better'n what ya git in the army," Billy informed the others.

"I don't give a hoot what they feed us a long as I don't eat no bullets," James Stepp added.

Billy Long considered all the talk and wondered about what they had been told. "You won't be doin' no fightin'," Whitaker had said with confidence. He figured Whitaker was telling the truth as he knew it, but did he really know? That was a question that lingered in Billy's mind as the group of recruits dealt with their first morning away from home.

The boys helped the postmaster that day. They cleaned the stable, swept the porches front and back, and cleaned all the windows. By midafternoon there was nothing for them to do so they waited and watched.

Whitaker came by that evening and informed them that they would be heading toward Asheville first thing in the morning but would stop in Fletcher the next day.

That night the boys got yellow-eyed beans and cornbread from the jailer. They all ate heartily and commented on how good the cornbread was. They lay around the stable that night and talked about everything from war to girls.

David Heatherly claimed to have kissed one of the Hollingsworth girls but had to recant when her brother threatened to hit him over it.

"I ain't never kissed a girl but I'd sure like to," James Stepp confessed.

Billy listened to all the talk but didn't say much. He and Tom Smith stayed to themselves. They'd grown up together and attended Edneyville Baptist Church all their lives. They had hiked and hunted all over Bearwallow Mountain together and were already close friends.

When they put out the lantern that night Billy and Tom lay side by side. "Hey, Billy, ya reckon Whitaker's tellin' the truth 'bout us not fightin' and all?" Tom asked.

"I reckon he's tellin' the truth best he knows it. But what I can't figger is how he knows what they'll do with us once they leave us in Asheville," Billy said.

"Yeah, me neither. And who's to say we'll be stayin' in Asheville? We've only been in Hendersonville two nights and we're movin' on," Tom said.

"You reckon we're gonna win this war?" Billy asked Tom as if he thought he might have some insight.

"I don't know, but Paw says so. But he worries about it all the time, like he might not believe it."

"Yeah, my Paw's the same way. He says we got to win it, on account of what they'll do to my sisters and Maw if the Yankees ever come here," Billy said.

"I don't wanna kill nobody but I reckon I will if I have to. They say it ain't no different than killin' a rabbit or a deer or somethin'," Tom added.

Neither of them thought much of their conversations. The next thing they recognized was the voice of the old postmaster, John Ward.

"Git up, boys, be ready to go, or I should say march. You'll be soldierin' soon. Whitaker will be here to fetch ya," he shouted as if he were the officer in command.

Whitaker came by and rounded up the boys. There was no wagon this time and they were informed that they would be walking to Asheville. They followed along behind Whitaker's horse as they made their way down Main Street toward the Asheville road. A few townspeople watched as they passed. It was a pathetic sight—a group of farm boys walking off into the unknown perhaps never to return.

They passed a smattering of traffic as they walked. There were freight wagons going this way and that. Sometimes people would speak to them; others would simply stare.

"Good luck, men," one old man shouted as he passed going in the opposite direction.

It seemed strange to Billy that he would call them "men." He still didn't think of himself that way.

Tom Smith walked along beside him. When the old man called them men Tom looked over at Billy and smiled as if to say he liked it.

When they got to Fletcher they were escorted to Calvary Church. The church had been used as a Confederate barracks since the beginning of the war. Many men had camped there and this group of boys would follow in their footsteps.

A spring rain had started so they were moved indoors to sleep in the church sanctuary. Two more boys had joined the group, one off Cane Creek and one off Hoopers Creek.

The church parishioners brought them a supper of real meat that came from the nearby Blake farm. The boys were all starved from the day's walk so all of them ate with an obvious sense of urgency.

They warmed by the fire as they chatted and speculated as to what their future held.

"I'm proud to be doin' this," one of the newcomers announced to the group. "We're gonna be there when the war is won. It'll be a day to tell our children about."

"That'd be a fine thing," Tom told Billy. "To see 'em Yankees surrender, I mean."

"Yeah, I reckon so, if ya don't git shot or nothin'," Billy added.

The church people brought them breakfast in the morning and the eating was good. They had bacon biscuits and plenty of milk.

"So far I reckon the eatin' is pretty good," Billy said. "I bet it don't stay this good, though."

Whitaker had left them the previous night. This morning a new leader who wore a genuine Confederate uniform greeted them. His name was John C. Edney. He had been in the real army and had fought in real battles. He was on detachment duty because most of his Sixty-fourth Infantry regiment had been captured at Cumberland Gap the previous fall. He'd been home on furlough so the Yankees didn't get him. His new duty was at home now and he called the boys together. He was a nephew of Captain Balis Edney and a native of Henderson County. He knew the Henderson County boys and felt a kinship to them.

"Men," he said. When Billy and Tom heard the word "men," they looked at each other and smiled. "We'll be marching to Camp Patton in Asheville today. It's a long way so we'll be keepin' a good pace the whole time. Git your gear together; we'll be movin' on soon."

All the boys grabbed their bedrolls and gathered in the yard. Edney thanked the church people and finished some rarely available coffee they'd given him. He climbed on his horse and rode up to the cluster of youthful soldiers.

"Follow me," he said as if they were marching into battle.

They walked long and hard all morning. They passed many well-wishers on foot, on horseback, and on wagons. A sense of pride began to develop among them as people tipped their hats or gave them a wave.

"God bless ya young men," one old woman shouted with passion.

"God save the South," her companion shouted after her as they passed in an old wagon driven by a slave.

When they arrived in Asheville there was more traffic and more soldiers in Confederate gray. The last part of their journey was a hike up South Main Street where so many Confederate soldiers had marched before them.

Soon they crossed the square and passed the courthouse. Some of the boys had never been to Asheville and to them the busy square and the constant traffic were impressive sights.

When they arrived at Camp Patton just northeast of town it was less exciting. Thousand of soldiers had passed through the camp before them. There was mud from the previous rain and a stench in the air. Many latrines had been dug and covered in the years prior, some still open or only partially covered.

There were tents about but they were tattered and worn. They were taken to a block of tents where Edney instructed them further. "You'll bed down here. Two to a tent and no fightin' over it."

Preston Lane and David Heatherly claimed the best-looking tent immediately. Billy and Tom examined the others apprehensively.

"We'll be gettin' more men from the western counties tonight," Edney said. "In a few days we'll be makin' the march to Camp Vance in Morganton. You'll be gettin' uniforms and weapons there."

Billy and Tom picked a tent and crawled inside. It was dark and damp with an odor so strong it twisted their faces. They crawled back out as the others considered their quarters.

"I don't know if I can sleep in there," Tom said with desperation in his voice.

Billy didn't hear him for he was watching the sad procession coming up the road toward the camp. It was another group of seventeen-year-old boys who'd been conscripted under the new law. They were from Haywood, Jackson, Macon, Clay, and Cherokee counties, all in the far western part of North Carolina.

The group was escorted by John Carver, another locally famous Confederate soldier. Carver was in the most famous cavalry unit in the entire war. He was a member of Wade Hampton's brigade of J.E.B. Stewart's cavalry. He rode with General Lee and was wounded seven times in a single battle. Carver was also a Henderson County Confederate.

Billy Long studied them as they followed the storied cavalryman into camp. They looked hungry and more frightened than his group from Henderson, Polk, and Transylvania counties. Not one of the boys had shoes. One of them stood out among the others. He had dark skin and a ponytail of coal black hair tied behind his head. His eyes were dark and his face seemed to carry no expression. He was not very tall but he looked lean and strong.

Billy had seen members of the tribe before but not very often. The proud young man with the long jet-black hair was a Cherokee Indian. The other boys in the group appeared lost and afraid, but the young Cherokee seemed unaffected.

An old woman came by and passed out chunks of hardtack and pointed to a water barrel. The new recruits scrambled for tents as Billy and Tom ate the last of their food from home.

"Take ya tins and git ya water thar," the old woman shouted to them without emotion.

Billy looked at Tom with obvious disgust and whispered to him, "I reckon we're in the army now."

Chapter Seven

—— JUNE 1, 1864 ——

Asheville, North Carolina
There was a soft, cool breeze passing through the ridges around the camp. A delicate orange hue formed behind Beaucatcher Mountain as the first light of morning touched the sky over Asheville. Robins chirped and a rooster crowed in the distance.

Young Billy Long lay fully awake, thinking of his home and family. He wondered about his little brother John and how he'd fare. John had never known a day when his older brother was not by his side. He anguished most over thoughts of his mother and that terrible day he'd been taken away.

There had been considerable delay at Camp Patton and the days passed painfully as if in slow motion. Edney had taught them to march using sticks for rifles. They seemed to practice the same routine over and over. Boredom had so overtaken the boys that they were impatient for the march.

Billy stirred from his tent and stepped into the dim morning light. There were others about as the camp awakened from its restless sleep. He could smell the fires and feel the gentle breeze as he walked among the tents.

Billy saw the young Cherokee sitting by the fire. He walked over to him and sat on the log beside him. The young man looked at Billy without speaking, without expression.

"Howdy," Billy said quietly.

The young man looked back but only nodded.

"I reckon you're an Indian, ain't ya?" Billy said knowing the obvious answer to his own question.

There was no response at first. Then he looked at Billy as if he were a fool and nodded. "*Sho*," he said as he looked away.

"We'll be marching to Camp Vance in Morganton soon. Did you know that?" Billy said searching for some response. "It's four or five days hard walkin', they say."

"I know this," the Cherokee responded.

"It's a real army training camp. We'll get uniforms and guns," he told his new acquaintance. "I've seen some Cherokees before but you're the first I've talked to."

"I'm not a Cherokee like others. I am Snowbird," the young man said.

"What's that? Snowbird?"

John Edney walked in on their conversation. He answered the question for the young man. "They're a different kind of Cherokee. They live on part of the Cherokee reservation but they consider themselves different," Edney said as he studied the young man closer. "They live way out in the mountains, in places where no white man has been yet. It's called the Snowbird Mountains. I ain't seen many of 'em myself."

Billy thought all this very interesting. Maybe the army wouldn't be so bad after all. He moved over beside the young man, extending his hand with a smile. "I'm Billy Long from Edneyville, in Henderson County. What's your name?" Billy asked.

The young Indian looked at Billy for a moment. Then he smiled. "I am Snowbird, from Snowbird Creek. I am John Rattler."

Chapter Eight

—— JUNE 1, 1864 ——

Greeneville, Tennessee
The winds of war had shifted as the reaper's wrath swept across the land. As the brave and committed slashed at each other probity guided their way, while the evil and the corrupt were guided by greed. For Lucifer's fold, there was advantage and opportunity amidst the smoke and flames of war.

By the summer of 1864 the mountains of southern Appalachia were filled with deserters and criminals of every description from both sides. Legitimate plans for recruiting from the north offered money, food, and shoes to all those who would join the Union army. But there was no reliable way to distinguish between the loyalist and the opportunist. Recruiters filled company ranks with men while filling their own pockets with stolen bounty.

Greeneville was a military camp in the summer of 1864. Union troops controlled the town and the people.

The Red Tavern was crowded with soldiers, camp followers, and women of the night. In the rear of the tavern men sat around a table taking their drink while playing poker. With games of this sort the winner was often the man who could outdrink the others.

Charles Hurtsell was a lieutenant in the Third North Carolina Mounted Infantry Union Regiment. A native of Washington, Tennessee, he'd operated as a small-time criminal with limited success before the war. Two of the seven men playing cards with him were Confederate deserters from North Carolina, but now they were privates in the Third North Carolina Union Regiment. Thomas Kirklenhall was from Henderson County, North Carolina, and Hinkly Morton was from Yancey County, North Carolina.

When the game ended Morton had beaten two Tennessee boys out of three "double eagles." These twenty dollar gold pieces were a small fortune in 1864. The losers were so drunk that they didn't notice cards coming from the bottom of the deck. Nor did they notice the departure of the three friends from Colonel George Kirk's regiment.

"Hey, Morton, ain't you sharin' that with ye friends? Ya is, ain't ya?" Hurtsell said with a sly laugh as they strolled down the street.

"Yeah, Morton, we're ya friends, ain't we?" Kirklenhall added.

"Hell no! I ain't givin' you uns a damned thing. We said when we went in thar we's playin' fer ourselves. Ya ain't changin' the game now," Morton told them while laughing aloud.

The trio turned down an alley where Morton stopped them.

"Here, Thomas, hold 'is here," Morton said as he handed him the bottle of rye whiskey he was drinking from.

Morton unstrapped his suspenders and pulled down his pants just slightly over his hips. He pulled up his shirt revealing a leather strap tied around his naked waist. The strap looped through a small leather pouch pressed against his abdomen. He took the three gold pieces and slipped them into the pouch. He tied the pouch tightly into place, then re-dressed himself.

"I reckon you boys'll be needin' some poker lessons," he said as he laughed and took the whiskey bottle back.

The three soldiers waddled and sang their way back to camp as they shared the bottle of rye whiskey.

CHAPTER EIGHT

Colonel George W. Kirk, commander of the Third Mounted Infantry, called several hand-picked officers into his tent and gave them the news. Before he began his speech he danced around with his hands in the air.

"Boys, we're fixin' to throw a hoedown! Only we ain't payin' fer it." He laughed vigorously as he continued.

The others in the room laughed with him anticipating something fun.

"I got us some orders from none other than Union General Alvan C. Gillem himself. We got spies in North Carolina and they done told me 'bout some fine pickin's.

"Lieutenant Hurtsell, bring 'at map. Let me show the boys where the pickin's is."

Hurtsell and Kirk spread a map out on a field table while the other officers of the regiment gathered around.

"Ya see now, 'em Confederate fools is runnin' outta men. So they figgers to fill in fer men with boys. Our spies say Colonel McRae and Colonel Mallet and the rest of the regular soldiers is bein' sent up to old Bobby Lee in Virginia. That means Camp Vance is guarded by nothin' but little boys cryin' fer their mamas." Kirk smacked the table and howled out loud as he told of his plans.

"One thing's botherin' me though, Colonel. Some of 'em boys can shoot better'n men. How we gonna keep 'em from puttin' up a fight?" one of the officers asked.

"Tell 'im, Hurtsell," Kirk said, laughing slyly.

"Well, ya see, fellers, our spies tell us they're still bringin' the little babies to the camp. They ain't been trained; they ain't even got guns. We gonna hit 'fore they gets any too," Hurtsell said with confidence. "Now here's the best part of all; we're bein' sent to destroy the bridge over the Yadkin River. That's what General Schofield is wantin' us to do. But real men with real guns guard it. It's fur into Reb country too. I ain't got much favor fer getting my ass shot on account of some damn bridge. Once we get thar, I say we just skip 'at nasty little job and leave after we raid Camp Vance. General Gillem don't care none, long as we takes care of him."

There were mumbles and talk of agreement and much discussion. The group settled down as Kirk raised his hand and continued describing his plan.

"Now, ya see, we gotta sneak down thar real quiet. I don't want no serious soldiers comin' after us 'til we're good 'n' done. Once we've done our business in the camp, then the hoedown can start on the way back." Kirk sneered as he looked around the table. "We'll rob ever sum-bitch 'tween here and Morganton!" The men in the tent all cheered at the prospect. "We'll kill any of 'em dumb Rebel lovers what gits in our way. I want everthin' we come across burned to the ground."

"Colonel, what about 'em Bible-totin' fools we got in the regiment? Ain't they gonna git in the way some, or go to tellin' somebody when we git back?" one officer asked in a worried tone.

"Don't ya fret none 'bout that. I ain't takin' the whole regiment. We're hand-pickin' just the right ones. The fellers that sees it eye to eye with the likes of us'll be goin'. No damn Bible-totin' do-gooders. Maybe 'bout a hundred twenty men," Kirk said. "Now here's somethin' else. General Gillem done got us fixed up with 'em new Spencer rifles, seven shot repeaters. If 'em Rebs gits after us comin' back up the mountains, we'll rain fire down on 'em." Kirk held up his hands as if he were firing a rifle, working his trigger finger repeatedly. "Now 'tween now and then, keep ya mouth shut and ya eyes peeled. We'll be marchin' in a few days."

Chapter Nine

―― JUNE 20, 1864 ――

Asheville, North Carolina
Camp Patton stirred with excitement and activity as the long awaited march was finally under way. The boys of the new Ninth Battalion of the North Carolina Junior Reserve were ready for assembly. They would be marching in formation but no sticks would be carried, as there were other more important items in hand.

The mostly silent John Rattler, Tom Smith, and Billy Long had become a trio of friends. They slept together, ate together, and marched together. They talked of home, girls, and war. For weeks now the three had been inseparable. They were so tired of camp life at Asheville that they were happy to be marching.

"Say, Billy, ya reckon we'll get far today?" Tom Smith asked as if he thought Edney might have told him something.

"I don't know, but if we don't march any faster than we got out of this camp we'll still be here a week from now."

"What do ya say, Rattler?" Billy asked with a sarcastic tone.

"Is no care to me. I go where go," he responded.

"I reckon I don't care neither as long as we get outta this dirty camp," Billy said.

The three young men rolled up their blankets with meager belongings inside. They stood outside their tent in the early morning light and waited for the call. Soon Edney's voice could be heard echoing over the hills. "Fall in men; form your companies."

Nearly two hundred youngsters from Buncombe, Madison, Henderson, Polk, Transylvania, Haywood, Jackson, Macon, Clay, and Cherokee counties fell into ranks as an official unit of the Confederate army.

Long, Smith, and Rattler fell into line side by side.

A large freight wagon carrying their supplies was pulled in front of the young men. Elevated slightly by the sloping lay of the land, the wagon offered Edney a suitable platform from which to speak. John Carver sat quietly in the saddle of his horse while Edney instructed.

"Men," he began, "you're now soldiers in the Confederate army. We're marching as far as we can go today so that we can make it to Camp Vance in five days."

Listening to Edney talk about it concealed the difficult reality involved. It was about one hundred miles from Asheville to Camp Vance. It would mean marching twenty miles a day. Most of the group of young recruits had no shoes.

"This march will prepare you for many marches to come fightin' this war. Know the men beside ya and learn to protect each other. A day will come when you may need one another to survive. Work hard and think fast. Move quick, 'cause if you don't you'll die.

"As soon as we get to camp you'll get uniforms and guns. Don't load 'em damn guns 'til you're told to. Too many men get shot in some damn fool accident. It happens all the time, so don't you be the one that kills himself before ya even see a Yankee."

Edney ended his speech and sat on the wagon seat beside the driver. Cavalryman Carver moved out front as the horses pulled the wagon to the front of the formation. The youthful procession began its slow crawl through Asheville and down South Main Street toward the Swannanoa River. Thousands of Confederate soldiers from western North Carolina had made the same trip many times in the years before. In the early days of the war the townspeople would gather on the streets and cheer them on singing "Dixie" as the men passed. Now people only stopped and stared as these boys marched by in visual testament to the state of the Confederate army.

The march along the Swannanoa took all of the morning and into the afternoon. By the time the procession reached Swannanoa Gap the boys were exhausted and sore. Some were bleeding from the feet.

Edney parked the freight wagon and stood on the side of the road urging the boys along. Slowly and painfully they climbed across the gap and started down the other side. Carver led them to the top and over the ridge. Eventually they stopped and camped along the creek above Old Fort in McDowell County.

Billy Long and Tom Smith complained aloud as the boys stripped and washed their tired and dirty bodies in the cool waters of the creek. John Rattler uttered no word of complaint. Preston Lane and David Heatherly, two boys from Henderson County, soaked their bleeding feet in the chilly mountain stream.

After they settled down by the fire Rattler pulled a small knife with a leather blade encasement from a secret pocket sewn on the inside of his pants. It had a small, thin blade only about four inches long, but the little handle was ornately decorated with beads and native stones. Rattler cut off parts of his fingernails as the boys stared at the fire.

"That's a mighty fine knife ya got there," Billy said.

"Is gift of father," Rattler said as he turned it from side to side. "Made good. Pretty, no?" he said as he handed it to Billy.

Billy took the knife and rolled it around in his hands. It was heavy for such a small knife but the beads and stones were perfectly arranged in the handle.

"Stones come from Snowbird Creek; beads come from white trader," Rattler said with a smile. "Is my family…with me, knife is. Protect me."

Billy handed it to Tom Smith and after a brief examination he returned it to Rattler.

"Father say always with me," he explained as he slid the knife back into the small pocket.

The three boys unrolled their blankets and bedded down for the night.

The hard marching continued for five more days as the boys were driven on by Edney, Carver, and their small cadre of veteran soldiers. The state of the boys with bleeding feet and exhausted bodies meant an extra day on the march, but the Ninth Battalion of the Confederate North Carolina Junior Reserves arrived at Camp Vance on June 26, 1864.

Upon arrival at the camp the enthusiastic Bob Roseman greeted the boys. He was energetic but tiny in physical stature. Bob was only fourteen but he'd been at the camp for months, long before the change in the conscription law. He was the camp drummer boy but he thought of himself as camp director.

He moved among the new arrivals like a traveling preacher. "Hey men, this here's Camp Vance. I'm the drummer, best damn drummer in the army. I know everything about this camp," he said with authority.

Roseman approached the trio of friends from the Asheville camp stopping and staring upward at Rattler. "Damn, he's an Injun, ain't he?"

Rattler stared back at him with indifference.

"Yeah, I reckon you're a smart one for figgerin' that," Billy said sarcastically.

Continuing with his demonstration of expert knowledge Roseman chattered on constantly about the camp. He led the boys to the rough sawed sheds that would serve as their barracks. He took them to the creek and led them to their latrines. He talked constantly, entertaining all who would listen.

"I'm gonna git to go with ya this time. They wouldn't let me go before on account of me being only thirteen but I'm fourteen now and the lieutenant says I kin go.

"I can't wait to git me a gun. That'll be somthin'."

CHAPTER NINE

"Hey, Bob, what ya gonna do with a gun? It'll be bigger than you are," Smith said as the others laughed.

"Who's gonna carry it fer ya?" another boy asked.

"Don't ya worry none 'bout me. I kin carry 'er and I kin shoot. I'm gonna shoot some of you uns in the ass first thing."

All the boys howled with laughter as they considered the threat. As a group they proceeded through the supper line getting a large cup of yellow-eyed beans and a big chunk of dry cornbread. After supper that night they all gathered around the campfire and listened with awe as Bob played the drum and sang the camp songs he'd learned.

The boys cheered him on as he enchanted them with a beautiful falsetto voice.

"Hey, Bob," Edney said, "if you'd sing more and talk less this world would be a heap better place."

Roseman only smiled as the other boys laughed. When the laughter abated he sang an old country hymn that brought back memories of home and family to all who heard it.

Billy pondered about all of his recent experiences and he reckoned that maybe things weren't so bad. He'd made new friends and he'd learned a lot. He bunked down that night feeling pretty good about things in spite of his aching feet.

The next morning the boys were rewarded for their efforts. Entertainment of a lifetime arrived in the form of a real train with a real steam engine, something none of them, except for Bob Roseman, had ever seen. They cheered and ran to the tracks as the train approached.

Billy and Tom screamed with delight as they ran along beside the slowing train. Rattler ran with them but kept a safe distance as he was uncomfortable with the big iron monster. Preston Lane grabbed onto one of the ladders and rode on a short distance waving with one arm as he went.

Roseman tried to keep up with them lecturing on all he knew about trains. But with all the noise and excitement little attention was paid to his expert dissertation.

"I can't wait to ride 'er," Tom announced as the train came to a stop.

"Me neither," Billy shouted behind him.

Rattler shook his head from side to side. He stared at the iron machine with trepidation. "Fight bear…better than ride iron train. Ride no good," Rattler said as the others laughed at his obvious fear of the loud machine.

"All right, men, ya get uniforms today and tomorrow ya get your guns," Edney yelled at them as they gathered around the train.

As the uniforms were unloaded from the train, the boys began trying them on at the railhead. Most of the boys were poorly dressed so the uniforms were the most exciting development of their brief military lives. Trades and swaps were made for over two hours until each boy was wearing the closest fit he could find. Still some fits were awkward.

Edney called them into formation and for the first time they felt like real soldiers. They stood in line with pants and jackets of a matching plain gray color. There were the consistent black stripes down the outsides of the pants and across the shoulders. The black stripes were the distinctive indication of a North Carolina Infantry soldier. There was one great disappointment, however; there were no shoes.

All the talk in camp that night was of getting their guns and the train ride to follow. Billy and Tom spent the evening talking and dreaming of where they would go from here. Rattler said not a word. He spent the entire evening sewing with borrowed needle and thread. After a tedious effort a small hiding place was created on the inside of the left thigh of his pants for storing his treasured knife.

Chapter Ten

—— JUNE 25, 1864 ——

Greasy Cove, Tennessee
Colonel Kirk led his blue-uniformed soldiers up to the three large freight wagons parked along the edge of the road. On many occasions these men were without mounts and this raid would begin the same way as most. Several horses had been taken in a raid across the North Carolina line earlier providing mounts for Kirk and a few others. Men in blue climbed the wagons and broke open the crates. They passed out the brand new Spencer repeating rifles to every man. Soldiers took their rifles then moved to the next wagon where they pick up ammunition pouches and one hundred fifty rounds of ammunition each.

Kirk's band was made up almost entirely of men from east Tennessee and western North Carolina. All of them were Confederate deserters and they all knew the mountains well. Of the six hundred men who joined the third North Carolina Mounted Infantry Union Regiment these men were the roughest of the lot. All had killed before and thought little of killing again.

Hunted by Confederates they had joined the Union not just for money and advantage but also protection from arrest. These were hard men now armed to the maximum with the most modern weapon of the war. Though there were only one hundred and twenty-five men in the force it was a formidable little army. Reliable spies assured them that there was no sizeable Confederate force outside Salisbury or Asheville except for two hundred unarmed boys at Camp Vance. Approximately fifteen armed adult males were all that stood between them and the capture of the camp.

Kirk gathered his men for one last talk before the march. "We'll move fast and shun the roads. Keep to the woods at all times and no jabberin' among ya. There'll be plenty to mouth 'bout when ya git back."

The motley band began a quick march with advance pickets staying out in front between a tenth and two tenths of a mile. If civilians or riders were spotted the entire band took to the woods. They crossed the high country at Roan Mountain working their way along trails above or beside the main roads.

Just across the state line they met up with their guide Joseph Franklin. Franklin was a Confederate deserter turned spy for the Union. Best of all for Kirk and his band of raiders was that Franklin was a native of Burke County. He'd been at Camp Vance and knew the lay of the land as well as the layout of the camp.

On the morning of June 26 they crossed the Toe River near Linville. Two young Huskins boys fishing along the river saw the small army as they crossed. Upon returning to town they reported the sighting. Two riders went out to investigate and found nothing. It was assumed that the boys were imagining things. There was no Confederate alert.

Kirk and his men worked their way down the Linville River, then crossed Upper Creek and found their way into Burke County by the night of June 27. Now only twelve miles from Morganton Kirk decided to march all night. He had evaded detection up to this point and since he had no intention of following his orders to burn the bridge over the Yadkin River the camp was his only real objective.

As he proceeded through the night Kirk laughed to himself. He knew the camp would be easy pickings and he also knew what an uproar his raid would cause.

He turned to Lieutenant Hurtsell as the two rode along together in front of the men on foot. "Ain't one damned soul gonna remember 'at bridge after they sees my name in all 'em Rebel papers. I'll be as high 'n' mighty as one 'em damn generals," Kirk said laughing quietly.

"I don't give a damn 'bout 'em papers. Ya just better not git my ass shot, is all I kin say," Hurtsell whispered back.

Kirklenhall and Morton marched directly behind the two as they worked their way through the night. "I hope to hell 'em two knows what they're doin'," Morton told Kirklenhall.

"Me too; I reckon it's the hoedown comin' back I want in on. I jus' soon leave 'at damn camp alone," Morton responded as he adjusted the leather pouch tied around his waist.

"Don't worry. Colonel Kirk ain't in for no serious fightin'."

The darkness shrouded the raiders as they got closer to Morganton. Within a mile of the camp they were still undetected.

Chapter Eleven

―― JUNE 28, 1864 ――

Camp Vance, Morganton, North Carolina
Billy Long lay restless in his bunk. "Hey, Rattler, are ya awake?" he whispered. "I didn't sleep none."

"No sleep. Bad wind blow from train," Rattler replied.

Billy wondered what he meant by bad wind as he thought about home and honey apple pie. As he pondered he heard noise coming from the awakening camp. He knew Rattler was uncomfortable with the strange monster of a machine they called a train. Of the two hundred boys at the camp Rattler was the only one who didn't want to ride it.

Just before dawn the boys could hear camp drummer Bob Roseman beating on his drum accompanied by an adult bugler. Roseman was good on his drum but the bugler only attempted to play something similar to reveille. Noise came from his bugle but there was little chance of identifying the tune.

"Time to get up boys," Tom Smith shouted to his two friends.

As they moved about the shed that served as their barracks Rattler tapped Billy on the shoulder and pointed toward the rear of the barracks with a strange look in his eye.

"Noise no good. Bad," Rattler said in a quiet voice.

No one noticed him as they continued with their routine except for Billy Long. He had learned to respect his quiet native friend.

"What noise?" Billy asked as he tried to listen.

Tom Smith joined the two as Billy tried to figure out what Rattler was talking about. Just as Roseman finished his drumming and the reveille ended Tom and Billy both heard the rustling of feet outside the back of the barracks.

"What was that?" Tom asked Billy and Rattler cocked his hear.

Billy crept over to one of the bunks, stood on it, then peered out one of the high windows. He turned back to face his two friends. There was terror in his eyes.

He rushed back to the other two. "Oh God, it's Yankees! They're sneakin' around the camp! Hundreds of 'em."

No sooner had Billy said the words than reveille was struck up for a second time, but there was no drum accompaniment. It sounded different and came from a different direction. Then there was shouting and rushing about in the camp yard.

Billy motioned to his friends for them to follow him to the back of the barracks. "Come on, y'all, we gotta run for it," he whispered as he looked out the rear of the building.

Billy jumped over the three steps that led to the ground and dashed for the woods some twenty yards behind the structure. Rattler and Smith were right behind him as they made their escape. As he passed a cluster of bushes at the edge of the clearing he was slammed in the stomach with a rifle butt and knocked to the ground. As he caught his breath Billy Long looked up to see a dirty, ragged man in a new blue uniform pointing a strange-looking short-barreled gun right at his face.

"Git ye ass up, Reb. I just as soon blow a big hole in yer face as look at ya." The man smiled displaying a set of rotten teeth. As Billy struggled to his feet he saw other soldiers in blue holding guns on Tom Smith and John Rattler.

As others were being rounded up they heard horses ride into the camp yard. They were marched around to the front of the barracks to see Confederate camp commander Lieutenant Walter Bullock standing in front of a cluster of Union soldiers on horseback. The Yankee leader was holding a large white flag of truce. Bullock seemed to be discussing something with the Yankee leader but they could not hear what was being said. Some of the adult Confederate soldiers stood with guns pointed. Several others in gray stood between the barracks with rifles pointed. A few more had hidden among the trees at the edge of the woods.

After a few minutes of discussion Bullock called Edney and two other Confederate men over to confer.

Bullock went back to the Union soldiers for more discussion. Then the adults came into the yard and announced that terms had been reached.

The boys had all been called into the center of the yard, where Bullock addressed them. "Men, we are surrounded by two regiments of Union soldiers, over two thousand men. I have negotiated terms for the surrender of the camp. All they want is the camp and the arms that are stored here," Bullock said with relief. "All of you are to get your bedrolls and gather in the yard. You are all paroled, provided we turn in all our guns. Once they're assured that our arms are turned in we can leave. You are under orders to obey the terms."

Soldiers in blue could be seen all around the camp and among the trees. The boys and their adult leaders went back into the barracks and gathered their things. As Billy rolled up his blanket he looked at Rattler.

Rattler returned the glance and shook his head negatively. "No good," he said in a low voice.

Rattler motioned for the back of the building as if to suggest that they run for it again. All the boys were terrified and Billy was afraid to try it. Besides, they were under orders.

When the assembly in the yard was completed all the boys stood in formation. The adult Confederates came forward and stacked their guns before the Union colonel, then returned to their formation. Billy looked around and noticed that substantial portions of the two hundred boys were missing. He realized that some must have made it to the woods during the early morning scramble.

Colonel Kirk whispered something to Hurtsell. Hurtsell gathered a group of men, who closed in on the helpless Confederate formation and surrounded them with guns pointed.

"Now you uns here. I'm Colonel George W. Kirk, United States Army, and this here camp belongs to me." He laughed. "Now you boys be good like yer mamma done told ya and I'll let ye go when I gits done with my work." Kirk cocked his head as he spoke, then smiled.

Kirk then gestured to Hurtsell. The Union officer called for more men, who began looting the buildings. Then they lit torches and proceeded to run among the buildings and set them on fire. Billy looked beyond Kirk and he could see smoke coming from the train depot, which had already been torched. Within minutes every structure at the camp was on fire.

Other soldiers came among the Confederates and searched the adults. A small revolver was found and taken from John Edney by Kirklenhall.

"Now what was ya doin' with 'at pistol, Reb?" Kirklenhall said as he examined it.

Without warning Kirklenhall put the pistol in his belt, then whirled around and slammed Edney in the jaw with his rifle butt. Edney was knocked to the ground and blood spurted from his mouth. He managed to struggle to his feet but clearly his jaw was broken and some of his teeth were knocked out.

Billy heard the Confederate commander ask Colonel Kirk when they could leave.

"Not 'til we're done," Kirk responded.

The looting and torching went on for over an hour when Lieutenant Hurtsell returned and reported to Kirk. Kirk turned to the cluster of prisoners revealing a wide grin. "Well, ya see here, fellers. I been thinkin' on this here situation. It's come to me 'at maybe some of 'em Rebs be less likely to come shootin' me in the ass if I was to have some their babies 'tween me and them." The other Union soldiers burst out laughing at the announcement. "'Sides, some of ya stumpheads is likely to come traipsin' after us if I was to let ya go. So I got a little surprise fer ya. I'm takin' ya on a holiday.

"You're all under arrest! You're now my prisoners. You'll stay under arrest and under guard unless pardoned or exchanged." Kirk laughed as he finished his speech.

Bob Roseman was standing just in front of Billy. He'd been mumbling and talking to himself but Billy paid little attention to it.

"You're a dirty, lyin' bastard," Roseman shouted at Kirk.

The men in blue all laughed aloud. Kirk walked over to Roseman and chuckled. "Are ye a boy or a mouse?" Kirk asked with a sneer on his face.

"Go to hell," Roseman responded.

Kirk laughed again, and then summoned Hurtsell. "Lieutenant, this little mouse ain't learned what his momma teached him about bein' proper. How's about ya give 'im a little lesson."

Roseman shouted again, "Go to hell."

Hurtsell slapped Roseman across the face. The drummer boy turned to speak again but before he could say another word, Hurtsell punched him in the stomach. Roseman doubled over in pain. "Now any more of you mouses got anythin' to say?"

More Union soldiers came among the prisoners with long pieces of rope. The boys were ordered to line up as the rope was looped around the waist of one, then extended six or eight feet to the next one. Other men tied the boys' hands together with short pieces of rope. Soon there were many lines of eight to ten strung together. Billy Long, Tom Smith, and John Rattler were tied together in a line behind Bob Roseman and John Edney. Some of the boys began to sob as they realized they were being taken prisoner. The war had been raging on for over three long years. All of them had heard of the horrors found in Union prisons.

Lieutenant Bullock began to protest, citing Kirk's promise of parole. Kirk laughed out loud, then turned to his men. John Carver had been waiting for the guard who was watching his group to turn his back. When the moment was right Carver shoved him to the ground and dashed for the woods. Young Preston Lane reacted within a split second and took off after him. The two were only a few feet from the shelter and cover of the forest when one of the Union guards fired off a quick shot from a kneeling position. The bullet hit Carver in the center of his back. He fell to the ground face-first and died within minutes. Preston Lane ran past the slumping Carver and disappeared into the woods as bullets whizzed by his head.

Bullock shouted in protest as the stunned prisoners watched the horror of Carver's death. Billy's thoughts of escape were wiped away by what he witnessed.

"You double-crossin' liar," Bullock shouted.

"Hey, fellers," Kirk said as he addressed his own men. "This Reb says we double- crossed him, says we ought to let 'em go. I's kinda figgerin' on it and wonderin' what you uns think." Kirk laughed again. "Let's take a vote on it. All you uns fer lettin' 'em go, holler yea. All fer takin' 'em fer a little hike, hollar nay."

There was a unanimous shout of "nay" from Kirk's men, followed by lots of laughter.

"Well, ya see thar, Reb. I done it fair and square. You had ya day in court and the jury done found ya guilty." Kirk and his men continued with laughter and calls of "guilty."

"All right, men. Move 'em out," Kirk called, and the strange procession began to move from Camp Vance heading northwest.

Chapter Twelve

—— JUNE 29, 1864 ——

Winding Stairs, North Carolina
Pillars of smoke and a growing number of Confederate escapees from Camp Vance alerted the surrounding communities and the town of Morganton. Exaggerated reports concerning the size of the raiding force and distance to the camp delayed Confederate response.

Kirk and his local spies knew that troops would have to come from Asheville or Salisbury. They also knew that there was no railroad from Asheville; he concluded that the most likely response would come from Salisbury. Kirk calculated that it would take at least a day or two for an organized move against him. He planned his escape accordingly. They would return to the Tennessee mountains, back to the safety of Union lines on approximately the same route.

Billy Long had difficulty keeping his balance as his hands were tied and he was tethered to a boy in front and one behind. The string of prisoners kept up as best they could behind Edney at the front of the line. Billy and his group were among the closest to the front of the retreating party. The Union soldiers pushed, prodded, and cursed them as they moved. Kirk rode up and down the line as the long procession snaked along toward the mountain passes.

Small raiding parties were directed to every house and farm as they passed. Private citizens were beaten and robbed. As a party of raiders was leaving the home of Robert Pearson he managed to shoot and kill one of them. Billy and his party passed the home of Confederate hero Samuel Tate as it was being looted and torched. As they crossed the Catawba River Billy thought he would drown as Roseman and Smith fell, pulling the others into the water. More Confederates escaped at the end of the procession as the raiders and prisoners struggled to cross the stream.

Billy turned to look at Rattler as they were herded along. "We're in deep trouble," he said, gasping for breath.

Rattler looked back with a steely gaze. "Bad wind," he said without emotion.

Roseman continued to shout insults at Kirk and the other raiders, his squeaky voice barley audible above the noise of the march. "Ya gonna pay fer this. Our men'll kill ever damn one of ya."

Edney turned repeatedly to shout at the drummer boy, squeezing the words through his painful jaw and damaged mouth. "Shut up, Bob! Ya ain't doin' nobody any good. Shut up, damn it!"

Lieutenant Hurtsell rode by as Roseman shouted at him. "You'll pay in hell, ya bastard."

Hurtsell stopped and laughed. "Hey, Morton. I believe this here little mouse started the whole damn war by himself."

Kirklenhall and Morton were now mounted with commandeered horses. Both men laughed as Hurtsell continued to agitate the drummer boy.

"Hey, mouse, ya done got caught in a trap, ain't ya?" Kirklenhall said as the others chuckled.

Roseman stumbled and sobbed as he went. He screamed more insults but they were inaudible.

"Hey, mouse, ya better watch that black Injun behind ya. They eat mice, ya know," Morton said as he stared at Rattler.

Rattler saw his stare and directed his eyes to the ground.

CHAPTER TWELVE

Morton spoke to him directly. "I ain't never cared for no dark-skinned Injun no way," he said with contempt in his voice.

Small raiding parties continued to spin off and rob and burn as they went. Intermittent gunfire and occasionally a screaming female could be heard in the distance. No civilian along the route was spared.

Rear pickets and local spies reported to Kirk on a regular basis. It was apparent that no sizeable force had been organized to pursue the raiders. The caravan of bedraggled soldiers, spies, and prisoners was halted for the night at the foot of Jonas Ridge, about fifteen miles northwest of Morganton.

Kirk organized his men in a large clearing at the foot of Winding Stairs. Pickets were posted along the south side of his camp and the prisoners were collected into a cluster at the center of the clearing, with his troops placed as guards in a circle around them. Small raiding parties went off into the darkness to do their bidding on unsuspecting civilians.

The prisoners loosened their ropes and lay on the bare ground but there was little sleep.

Edney gathered his little group and whispered quietly through clenched teeth and broken jaw. "If ya get any chance, run for it. Do it, they might shoot ya but goin' to a Yankee prison'll be 'bout the same."

Billy, Tom, and Rattler huddled close together but said little as they waited through the night. They tried to sleep but Roseman sobbed and cursed constantly, disturbing all around him. There was also a constant coming and going among the Union raiders.

When the sun finally began to peek above the horizon the soldiers in blue worked among the prisoners checking and rebinding the ropes around the prisoners' waists and hands. Kirk prepared to organize his caravan for the trek up into the mountains. As the process was near its end, Union pickets came running into the camp.

"Rebs! Rebs!" they shouted.

"Rebs comin'! Lots of 'em!" They pointed toward the southeast as they hurried into camp.

Bob Roseman immediately began to scream and shout. "I told ya, ya damn Yankees is gonna hang. Ever damn one of ya."

Kirk was now mounted giving orders to all his men. Lieutenant Hurtsell conferred with Kirk and Billy could see a wide grin come over the lieutenant's face. He called his men together hurriedly directing them to round up the prisoners. Billy and the others were pushed and prodded toward the Winding Stairs where Kirk was positioned at the lower end.

Kirk pointed left and right as his soldiers followed his instructions. Hurtsell began to shout out the orders. "String 'em along here, and here. Tie their hands to tree limbs. Face 'em toward the Rebs!"

Billy looked at Tom and Rattler with an expression of fear when he realized what was happening. Soldiers in blue dragged groups of roped boys in lines across their front and began throwing ropes across tree limbs. Other soldiers went up and down the line tying the hanging ropes around the boys' hands. Then they pulled them, with arms stretched up, toward the tree limbs, then tied them off. Within minutes Kirk had a human shield of boys strung out several hundred feet in front of his lines.

"Alright men, now y'all lay down all along behind 'em babies," Kirk shouted.

Men in blue positioned themselves behind the line of hanging boys. They cocked their Spencers and waited as the last of the pickets came in with sporadic gunfire popping behind them.

Waightsill Avery, a Morganton lawyer, and Captain George Harper, a Confederate Home Defense officer, led over three hundred Confederates in pursuit of the raiders. As the rescue party approached the area below Winding Stairs the men in blue opened fire. The Confederates coming out of the woods below were soon returning fire.

Bullets whizzed in all directions as more Confederates came up. Billy and the other boys struggled to free themselves as they dangled from the ropes. The Union soldiers were well positioned behind logs and rocks with the prisoners protecting their front.

Bob Roseman screamed encouragement to the Confederates.

CHAPTER TWELVE

Lieutenant Hurtsell, Hackley Morton, and Kirklenhall were together behind a rock.

Kirk looked at the trio and pointed at Roseman. "Shut that little bastard up."

Hurtsell raised his Spencer and sighted in on the drummer boy's lower back as he dangled from a tree limb. He squeezed the trigger and there was a loud pop. The bullet pierced Roseman's back at a thirty-degree angle, clipping the spine and exiting through his lower abdomen. The force of the round tore open the front of his tiny body spilling his innards through the gaping exit wound.

Roseman turned to Billy and stared as Billy looked back in horror. The little drummer boy tried to speak but instead of words, blood spewed from his mouth. Billy screamed in panic and struggled against his ropes. Roseman's eyes closed and his head drooped as his last breath left his body.

Hurtsell turned to Norton laughing and shouting. "Hey, Norton, I can't hear that little shit no more. I reckon he's done. Why don't ya git that Injun while we're at it."

Morton just smiled and raised his rifle. He pointed it to the center of John Rattler's back and leveled his sights. There was a distant report as Confederates moved in toward the Union left. Just as Norton was about to pull the trigger a Confederate ball struck him in the left eye killing him instantly. As he fell away he pulled the trigger instinctively but the shot flew harmlessly into the trees.

As more fire rained back and forth several of the prisoners were hit. Avery made his way up to the front to determine the Union strength and position. As he approached the front of the tree line he shouted in near panic. He began to shout as loud as he could. "Stop! Stop! Hold your fire! They've got our boys out front!"

Avery screamed and shouted as the word was passed. Many Confederates could not hear so Avery waved his arms as he shouted. In the urgency of the moment Avery had left the safe cover of the trees. As he signaled to his men he was shot down and killed.

For a while the soldiers in blue continued to fire. One more boy was hit in the back of the leg. Soon the Confederates stopped firing completely and slowly fell back into the trees. A few of the boys had managed to work free and run through a hail of bullets to safety.

Kirk recognized the opportunity knowing that several of the Confederates had been killed. He rode around shouting to his men while Hurtsell and Kirklenhall dragged Morton's body into the rocks. The two men tore at his pants, stripping him from the waist to the knees. Kirklenhall held the leather strap while Hurtsell cut it. The two men took the leather pouch and divided the gold.

Hurtsell smiled at Kirklenhall and spoke softly. "I reckon he ain't gonna need this money no way."

They rolled his body into the rocks and rejoined the Union caravan. The prisoners were hurriedly placed in line and the strange parade began marching up the Winding Stairs headed for Tennessee.

PART TWO

Chapter Thirteen

—— JULY 23, 1864 ——

Cairo, Illinois
Billy Long decided that he no longer favored a train ride. Since the capture at Camp Vance Billy had traveled a great distance. They were marched on foot to Greeneville, Tennessee, then put on a train with eighty men loaded in each open cattle car. His first train ride carried them to Chattanooga, Tennessee, not from Morganton to Raleigh as they had always expected. In Chattanooga they boarded a steamboat and headed west. The black soot belching from the train engine had covered the Confederate prisoners in Billy's car. At Cairo, Illinois, as they marched from the river landing to the train station the soot-coated Confederates cast a pathetic shadow. Despair and depression were visible despite their blackened faces as they trudged along with heads bowed.

Citizens of the town gawked at the parade of prisoners as they marched to the waiting rail cars. Billy thought of the dream he'd had while still at home. The visions of grand battles and even combat had crossed his mind but for this he was totally unprepared. Shame overcame him as passing soldiers cursed them and laughed at their miserable plight.

The weeks of travel had been hard on all of them but most of all John C. Edney. His broken jaw continued to bother him and there was no medical care available. After hours and days on trains and on the river all of them were exhausted. There had been little to eat and they often went thirsty between stops. What little sleep there was came on the ground in a makeshift transit camp or on the floor of a rail car.

Billy and Rattler helped Edney board the slatted cattle car as they prepared for the last leg of their journey to prison. At least this one was covered, Billy thought, as he helped Edney to a back corner in the filthy train car. The Junior Reserves from North Carolina were mixed with Confederate prisoners from all over the South, all boarding the train north. This was one of the busiest rail lines in the country during the war. The Illinois Central Railroad was always carrying hundreds of prisoner up and hundreds of head of cattle coming back.

Guards in blue uniforms prodded them into the cars until they were full. The large sliding door was closed and locked behind them. Billy sat beside Edney with his knees drawn to his chin. Rattler and Tom Smith crouched with them as they waited in silence.

Edney's jaw was blue and swollen but he carried on, leaning against the side wall and closing his eyes. Billy knew little or nothing about medicine but he knew Edney was in trouble. Soon there was the familiar knocking and jerking as the train began to move. Edney grimaced but he didn't cry out.

Billy stared out through the large gaps between the wooden slats. He remembered his dream of fighting honorably and being a hero. He was disgusted with himself now. He felt he had done nothing; he hadn't fought them, didn't even have a gun. Now Billy was going to a Union prison, a place that everyone said was hell on earth. It was in a city called Chicago where the winters were frozen and dark. It was a camp he'd never heard of until they boarded the riverboat. It was a place called Camp Douglas.

Billy thought it best to help Edney lie down. But there was another Confederate soldier sitting beside them. He was among several prisoners from Georgia captured in Mississippi.

"Hey, fella, can ya make room for me to lay him down there?" Billy said calmly.

"Yeah, I reckon so. But I ain't got much room," the man replied.

Temporarily deceived by the soot Billy did not notice that the man was not black from the soot but was of black skin. There were a number of such men in the Confederate army but Billy had only seen one in Henderson County. But here he was, a black man in a Confederate uniform on a train headed for a Union prison camp. Such service was against official policy of the Confederate government but individual commanders often waived the rules.

"My name's Billy Long; this here's Tom Smith and John Rattler."

Billy stuck out his hand and the young black man took it with a smile. "I be Isaac Marlboro of the Thirty-eighth Georgia. I ain't neva been up north. I is a might skeered of bein' cold. Ain't nothin' as bad as a man freezin' ta death," Marlboro said.

The group of young men twisted and shifted as they moved to accommodate a prostrate John Edney.

Rattler looked at Edney then back at Billy with the same calm stare. Then he shook his head from side to side. It was still July and the youngsters from North Carolina had not considered the cold of a place so far north.

"Skin hot. No good," Rattler whispered to Billy and pointed at Edney.

"Yeah, I know. The way his jaw is swelled up, I figure he's gettin' gangrene or somethin'," Billy said.

The train now moved at full speed across the vast Illinois farmland. Billy peered through the slats and marveled at the seemingly endless miles of green corn growing in the fields. His paw would sure like to see that, he thought, as he remembered his own hunger.

Billy and Rattler leaned against the sidewall and each other as the train rambled along. Billy closed his eyes and tried to sleep as he saw visions of his mother and home. Sadness overcame him as he faced the reality of where he was going and the ominous prospects of a future life yet to be determined. Sleep would not come as tears seeped from his closed eyelids revealing the emotion he had hoped to conceal. For the first time, Billy accepted that he might not ever hold his mother again, nor work the field with his father and brothers, nor hunt the highland pastures of Bearwallow Mountain.

Chapter Fourteen

—— JULY 24, 1864 ——

Chicago, Illinois
The Illinois Central Rail Road had constructed many spur rails in and around Chicago. It was a massive city of one hundred and ten thousand civilians in 1864. At any given time there were always thousands of blue uniformed soldiers coming and going in the city. Also there were as many as twelve thousand Confederate prisoners housed at Camp Douglas on the southeast side of the city.

The prison rail spur brought the rail cars within a few hundred yards of the prison gates. Clusters of guards in blue uniforms surrounded each train car and slid the doors open along the sides. The guards were members of the Fifteenth Veterans Reserve Corps.

"All right, ya dirty Rebel pigs. Scramble yer nasty asses off that train," one guard yelled as the door was opened.

Billy and Rattler lifted Edney with the help of their new friend Marlboro. Once on his feet Edney was able to walk with some difficulty. The men nearest the doors began jumping or dropping to the ground as others waited in groups behind them. Tom Smith and Marlboro jumped down first and waited as Billy and Rattler passed Edney to them.

Tom and Rattler stood on either side of Edney as Marlboro rejoined his Georgia group.

"Now, ya crackers, line yer asses up right along here," the Union soldier said as he gestured to a line in front of the train.

"My name here is Old Socks," the soldier in blue said with a sly laugh. "They calls me Old Socks 'cause 'ats what I does, sock people; that's if I ain't inclined to shoot 'em first."

As the rows of men formed Billy could see the Georgians forming in front of his group. Men in blue marched by with guns pointed at the prisoners. Old Socks marched up and down the formation clearly enjoying his authority over the prisoners. Suddenly he did a double-take and turned to glare at Marlboro standing in the second row.

"Land sakes alive! Damn if it ain't another one of 'em nigger Rebs," Socks said, then roared with laughter. "Goddamn, boy, you a dead ass nigger sho as sunrise."

Other soldiers in blue came for a look, then joined in the laughing and taunting.

Marlboro stared straight ahead and ignored all the words. Socks parted the front row and stood with his face inches from the black man's face. His demeanor shifted from humor to anger. "We hate niggers here, Reb niggers in par-tick-a-lar."

As the prisoners were moved toward the prison gates they marched past a group of dismounted Union cavalry soldiers. The soldiers taunted the prisoners and cursed them as they passed. Some of them picked up pieces of broken bricks that had been piled up along the road and tossed them at the Confederates. One of these bricks struck Tom Smith in the side of the head knocking him to the ground. Billy held onto Edney while Rattler picked up the stunned and injured Smith.

"Are ya alright?" Billy asked as the sad assembly continued along.

"Head bleed," Rattler said as he looked at the bleeding wound on the side of Smith's face.

CHAPTER FOURTEEN

After the Confederate prisoners passed through the gates at Camp Douglas they were marched into Prisoners' Square and ordered to stand in formation. A tall, bearded officer appeared and walked up the steps to a platform rising in front of the formation. He turned and stood facing the captives. "I am Colonel Benjamin J. Sweet and you are now under my command. There will be no toleration of prisoners who break the rules. If you break the rules you will be punished; if you try to escape you will be shot," the colonel said without emotion. "There are no more exchanges and rations for prisoners have been cut by order of Secretary Stanton. Any complaint will be met with harsh punishment.

"Now that we understand the rules I will offer you a chance to make amends for your sins. If you renounce your treason and take the oath of allegiance to the United States you will be allowed the privilege of joining the Union army," Sweet announced with cold indifference.

The prison commander and the Union guards got bonus bounty money for all recruits that came from the prison population. The prisoners got none of the bounty but they did get out of prison and into the Union army.

There was a pause for a few minutes as a quiet rumble passed through the Confederates.

Edney perked up on hearing this. He raised his head and looked at the others in his group with defiance etched on his broken face. "Hell no, ain't none of us goin' to the Yankees!" Edney mumbled through his broken jaw.

"If you join the Union army you'll get shoes, food, and pay in U.S. greenbacks," Sweet continued. "You'll be sent out west to fight Indian savages instead of fighting those other fools in the Rebel army."

Someone in the back row shouted, "Hell no, I won't swallow no dog fer you ner any other Yankee!"

Many others joined in the defiance. Shouts and gestures popped up intermittently as the prisoners rejected the offer. Billy Long found himself shouting along with the others. "Hell no, we won't join!" Billy shouted.

But some men, only a few, raised their hands. A few others began to step forward. Out of the three hundred men who came in on the train that morning two dozen took the oath and joined the Union army.

As the new Union recruits were marched toward the protection and segregation of different barracks in White Oak Square the other Confederates cursed and jeered at them. "Traitor! Traitor!" was the call from the other prisoners as the men marched away to segregated barracks and the promise of a full stomach.

Billy and the injured and bleeding Tom Smith shouted along with the other men. "Swallow the damn dog and choke on it," Smith called out as the last of the new Yankees disappeared.

"The rest of you fools will now march to your assigned barracks," Sweet said as he gestured to the lieutenant.

As Sweet walked away and the prisoners began to move Billy heard Socks call out to Red O'Hara, one of the prison's most ruthless guards. "Hey, Red, did ya see the nigger Reb?"

"No, whar's the nigger?" O'Hara shouted back.

"He's walkin' right at ya, in that bunch thar," Sock said as he pointed and laughed.

As each prisoner turned the corner to go around the first barracks building he faced in the direction of Red O'Hara's position on the guard line. O'Hara took a quick look, then raised his rifle and fired. The bullet struck Marlboro in the chest, tearing through the aorta and bursting through the back of his ribcage. Marlboro collapsed to his knees, then fell forward to the ground with blood spurting from the wound and his mouth. He was dead within seconds.

Colonel Sweet turned back to face the panic-stricken prisoners. "Well done. Excellent shooting I might add. See to it that soldier's rewarded for his excellent shooting, Lieutenant."

He looked at the prisoners and shouted for all to hear. "Welcome to Camp Douglas."

Chapter Fifteen

—— JULY 25, 1864 ——

Chicago, Illinois
The compound at Camp Douglas consisted of sixteen rows of buildings, four to a row. Each building was ninety feet long, twenty-four feet wide, nine feet high. Each of the prison barracks had two stoves and three levels of bunks. The prison was located in a low, swampy area close to the shore of Lake Michigan.

The North Carolina Junior Reserves were assigned to barracks number twenty-three. Others housed there were also from North Carolina. Among the few bright spots during their entire ordeal was the reunion with old friends and family from home. Camp Douglas contained a number of men from western North Carolina and Henderson County. One of the other prisoners was Marcus Long, Billy's brother.

When the new prisoners entered barracks number twenty-three there were immediate calls of recognition and warm greetings. When Billy saw Marcus among the men his emotions overcame him. The two men rushed to each other and embraced, something they had never done at home. Billy sobbed openly as Marcus fought back his own tears.

"Oh damn, Billy, no! Why are you here? I had hoped they'd never git ya," Marcus said as he stood staring at his little brother in disbelief.

"They changed the law. I got called as soon as I turned seventeen. Maw pitched a fit, somethin' awful," Billy said as he brought his tears under control.

Billy wiped his face and the black soot and tears smeared streaks across his cheeks. He looked at his older brother with deep concern. Marcus Long was drawn and emaciated. His lips were swollen and his teeth were gone.

"Lord, Marc, what have they done to ya?" he said as he began to cry again.

"Aw, ain't nothin', but they sez I got scurvy. The colonel cut off vegetables and fruit a long time ago. There's lots of us shrunk up like this," he said as if it were an acceptable circumstance.

"This here is my best friends. We got took by the Yankees all together and we been together since camp in Asheville," Billy told him as he introduced Rattler. "And you remember Tom Smith, don't ya?"

Marcus Long was a member of the Sixty-fourth North Carolina Infantry Regiment. The entire regiment had been captured in September 1863 at Cumberland Gap. Those who were still alive had been at the prison for nearly a year. Several Confederates from Henderson County had died.

Marcus walked Billy, Tom, and Rattler around saying hello to old friends and meeting new ones. He led them to a group of bunks where John Heatherly sat tending to two of his brothers. Aaron and Soloman were very sick and could not raise themselves to speak.

John Heatherly, Tom Smith, and Billy all knew each other from the past. They smiled and laughed as they talked of home. But John's joy was brief as he turned and looked at his two brothers. "They took five of us Heatherly brothers at Cumberland Gap. Pleasant and Squire are already dead and I don't think Aaron and Soloman will last much longer. They won't give us enough to eat and them crazy guards'ill kill ya just fer fun." He sobbed quietly as he told of the despair in the camp. "Now David is here too."

CHAPTER FIFTEEN

The Morgan brothers, John and Alfred, soon joined the small reunion. They were also from Henderson County. There were three of them, but their brother, also named Aaron, had died two months earlier.

Billy and Tom reported all they could remember regarding the news of home. Rattler just listened and said little as the conversation turned from reports of home to prison life.

Tom Smith asked why the sick Heatherlys were not in the hospital.

"The hospital stays plum full all the time," Alfred Morgan said. "It ain't good fer nothin' much no how. Ya get a little more to eat though. We gits more help from the townspeople and the students from the Baptist school next to the camp than we gits from the Yankee guards."

"Stay away from Socks and O'Hara," John Heatherly said. "They'll kill a feller fer nothin' but passing the time o' day."

"That Prairie Bull is just as bad; he'll shoot a man fer nothin' and they all like to beat and torture us," John Morgan said.

"If ya gets called to do any duty, just do what they sez. Don't talk none and don't never look 'em in the eye neither. They's just as likely to shoot a feller fer that as anything else," Alfred Morgan told them.

Heatherly pointed over to Edney, who was lying in a bunk across the room. "He don't look so good. What's wrong with him?"

"When we got captured at Camp Vance he was in charge of us. Some of Kirk's men hit him in the jaw with a rifle butt and busted out his teeth and broke his jaw. It's been getting' worse ever since," Billy said. "I'm afraid he's got it infected."

Billy and John Rattler shared a bunk above Edney and Smith. The heat of the day cooled down considerably that night and Billy had an extended sleep for the first time in days. He awakened to reveille, not sure what lay in store for the new prisoners. As they formed each day the guards selected prisoners for duty and the others were returned to the barracks.

On this day the new prisoners were picked. Their guards were two older men who seemed to have little interest in the prisoners or their duty. "Come along with us, Rebs," one of the two instructed.

"Is he a nigger?" the older guard asked as he looked at Rattler with suspicion.

Stricken with fear, Billy spoke up quickly. "No, no he's just an Injun, a Cherokee."

The guards seemed to accept the explanation and kept moving.

"Where're we goin'?" Tom Smith asked with his head still throbbing from the brick blow.

The guards stopped and looked at Tom as if he were an idiot.

"What ta hell does it matter to ya, Reb? Has ya got an appointment to tend to? Maybe yer goin' courtin' this evenin'," the older guard said sarcastically.

"Well, a feller needs to smell purdy fer courtin', so I reckon you'll take kindly to yer duty," the other man said with a chuckle.

The young Confederates were led to a small building at the end of Prisoners' Square. The guards opened the door and gestured for them to enter on their own. Immediately a rank odor engulfed them. Billy almost gagged as Tom and Rattler covered their mouths and nostrils.

The two guards stood at the door and laughed hysterically.

"Hey, Rebs, 'is here be the Dead House. Ya might as well git to know it best ya kin, seein' how you'll likely be here yourself one day," one guard announced as the other laughed.

The three boys stepped back as if hit by an ocean wave but the guards pushed them back in.

"Now, ya little shits, git this here. Ya gonna drag them dead bodies outta thar and put 'em on that wagon yonder." The older guard pointed to the wagon parked nearby. A strange-looking man in civilian clothes stood by the wagon and watched with a smile.

Billy could not believe his eyes. He'd never seen anything so horrible in all his life. Fourteen dead bodies lay side by side across the dirt floor that made up the Dead House. As the light hit the room large rats scurried off in all directions.

Billy and Tom stood motionless as Rattler spoke more than usual.

"Dead man stink, but no hurt. Move to wagon or join on floor," Rattler said calmly as he gestured toward the two guards who were now pointing their weapons at the trio.

It took a second or two for Billy to interpret what Rattler said but soon it added up. They stepped into the room as Rattler pointed to the first body on the end. Rattler stepped behind the dead man's head. He crouched down, placed his hands under the man's armpits, and lifted him up. Billy grabbed one leg and Tom grabbed the other. The three boys carried the stiffened cadaver some forty feet before placing it on the wagon and rolling it toward the back.

When they returned for another body Tom Smith cried out in horror as he looked at the face. It was Marlboro, the black Confederate murdered by Red O'Hara the previous day.

Tom covered his face with his hands as he spoke. "Oh God have mercy! The rats ate his ears off!"

"No look. Look no good," Rattler said as he moved behind Marlboro's head and picked him up on one end.

Tom sobbed as he and Billy picked up a leg and carried his lifeless body to the wagon.

When all the bodies were loaded onto the wagon the strange civilian walked up to the young Confederates and extended his hand with a broad smile on his face. "I'm C. H. Jordan, the camp undertaker. I sees to it these boys gits a fine burial. I'm just a small businessman, workin' fer my country. Yes, sir, I earns a fair wage fer my hard work," he said as he smiled. "Now you all just follow along behind the wagon and we'll git this duty done."

The macabre procession slowly wound along the camp boundary until they exited through the north gate. The boys walked behind the wagonload of corpses, and the guards walked behind the boys. After a considerable distance the wagon turned toward the lake, traveled along the shoreline, then pulled to a stop.

Jordan climbed down from the wagon seat and pointed at the edge of a ten- or twelve-foot cliff overlooking the western edge of Lake Michigan. He turned back to the boys and told them what to do. "Now ya just snatches up one of 'em, carry 'im over yonder, and pitch 'im in."

It was the most disgusting thing they had ever seen. None of the boys had ever been in battle so they were not hardened to death as many of the Confederate soldiers who had come to Camp Douglas were.

"Pull this way," Rattler said as he urged them on to complete their ghastly chore.

As they pitched the first body over Billy looked over the edge and saw other bodies bobbing in the waves. Many were partially decayed or partially dismembered from being battered on the rocks. Some of the corpses were covered with sand and silt; others were mostly skeletons. Gulls and other birds fed on the remains of some.

Billy's mind drifted as he thought of his dream. As they carried the stinking bodies one by one he remembered the images of grandeur and heroics that had danced through his mind. This war and his place in it were not what he had expected. The reality of war was not like his dream of glory but rather like a dream of darkness and despair, a nightmare of the most frightening nature. It was a nightmare that seemed to spin out of control, bringing torture and death to him and everyone around him. The worst of it was that this experience was not a dream; it was reality.

Chapter Sixteen

—— AUGUST 18, 1864 ——

Chicago, Illinois
Rumors spread through the camp that night. Someone had snatched camp guard Prairie Bull's dog. The prospects for such an animal among starving men were not good. Later that day one of the prisoners posted a note at the washhouse. It was just a simple poem:
> FOR LACK OF BREAD THE DOG IS DEAD.
> FOR LACK OF MEAT THE DOG IS EAT.

While a few Confederates may have enjoyed a meaty meal the aftermath was sure to be unpleasant. All the prisoners were called to formation in the Prisoners' Square.

Prairie Bull and Red O'Hara cursed and kick the men as they came out of the barracks and into formation. Other guards followed the example.

Bull waved his musket and screamed, "I'm gonna git the one who done it. Now one of ya better step out right now and tell who done this or you'll all pay to hell."

None of the prisoners moved or spoke. Bull and O'Hara walked up and down in front of the formation cursing and spitting on the prisoners.

"I'll git one of ya Rebel shits to talk, one way or t'other," Bull said.

Billy, Tom, and Rattler stood in line with other Junior Reserves in the second row. Fear gripped them all as they listened to the ranting guards. All the prisoners knew that one false move or a glance of the eye could result in death.

Colonel Sweet stood on the guard walk above the formation watching as the guards tried to extract the name of the perpetrator. After watching the scene unfold for several minutes without results the colonel called out to the guards.

"Sergeant O'Hara, someone must be punished for this crime. Select some prisoners and take them to the rack for punishment. If they tell you the name of the criminal you may shorten the punishment. If not, make it severe."

"Yes, sir, Colonel!" O'Hara yelled back to his commander.

Prairie Bull and O'Hara walked among the prisoners until they came to a stop in front of the Junior Reserves from North Carolina.

"Maybe some of these young uns is likely to talk," Bull said with a smile.

"Yeah, maybe so," O'Hara said as he stared at the youngsters.

O'Hara parted the line in front and selected the youngest looking members of the group. "You, and you there, step forward," he said as he pulled Tom Smith out by the shoulder and shoved him to the front.

"Git that black Injun too; I wanna see how he screams," Bull said with an evil sounding laugh.

Billy was the last of eight selected. They were placed in a line in front of the formation of prisoners, then marched to the other side of the camp. The gates were opened to a small enclosure where four wooden structures resembling oversized doorframes stood in a long row.

The guards called the boys forward one at a time and ordered them to stand under the wooden structures while they threw leather ropes over the top of the frame. Billy stood beside another boy in the frame behind Tom and Rattler, who were side by side.

Guards came to each prisoner and tied the thin leather ropes around the boys' thumbs until they were extremely tight. Then the ropes were thrown over the frame; the ropes were pulled until each boy stood with arms stretched to the sky with only the tips of their toes touching the ground. After stretching the ropes, they were tied off on hooks screwed into the frames.

"Now any of ya little bastards care to tell us who got that dog?" O'Hara screamed at them.

There was no response from any of the eight prisoners. Billy felt intense pain immediately. He tried to stretch further to relieve some of the pressure from his thumbs. The guards left them there for fifteen or twenty minutes while they ambled about enjoying a smoke and talking.

"Now we know ya fellers is kinda new here so we gives ya a little extry time to remember things. So if ya ain't remembered nothin' yet I reckon we can give ya a little rememberin' lesson," Bull announced, anger and contempt apparent in his voice.

Billy had heard of this torture from the older prisoners. He and all the others knew that hanging by the thumbs was only part of the plan.

"Please, sir, we don't know nothin', I swear to God," Billy cried out with fear.

"You're a lyin' little bastard, and I'll bet that's why yer momma sent ya off."

Billy closed his eyes and began to pray. He could hear one of the other boys mumbling a prayer behind him.

"Oh please, God, help me. Save me," Billy prayed silently as he prepared for the worst.

A number of the guards walked over to a pile; each man picked up a two-by-four, each about five feet long. They finished their cigarettes and talked nonchalantly as several of them walked into position behind the hanging boys.

O'Hara positioned himself behind Tom Smith while other guards moved behind the other boys. O'Hara started with the first swing. He moved the board back, then swung it forward with all his strength, lashing Smith across the back. Billy could see all of this happening right in front of him. Within a second or two he felt the first blows across his own back.

The guards continued to beat the prisoners as the boys sobbed and begged for mercy. Prayers were audible from Billy as the beating continued. He looked to the heavens through his tears as he recited the twenty-third psalm as best he could. He looked in front of him and watched as O'Hara aimed for the soft area below Tom's ribs striking him as hard as he could.

After an extended period of beating the guards were exhausted and sweating. The August sun added to the misery of the boys and their torture.

"Whew damn, honest work'll wear a man out," Bull said as he leaned on his two-by-four.

"Ya ain't shittin' me. This here is hard work," one of the other guards added.

Billy was still praying but through his prayers he could hear Tom sobbing. Not a word or sound came from Rattler but Billy worried for them both.

"God, please help them," he muttered through his own tears.

"Now if ya little shits knows somethin' ya best be spittin' it out right now. I don't take kindly to all 'is work," O'Hara shouted to the boys while the other guards continued with their rest.

"I reckon they likes this here game, don't you, Bull?" O'Hara said sarcastically.

"Yeah, I reckon so."

Some of the guards who had taken a seat began to get up and move back into position behind the boys. As soon as the movement started the boys began begging again and praying.

Billy could hear Tom Smith sobbing loudly and pleading with all emotion.

"Please, God, I'm hurt. Please stop. Oh God, Jesus…help me," Tom moaned.

O'Hara reeled and slammed the board across Tom's back. Then he reared again and swung lower. When the board hit, Tom screamed in agony. At the same moment blows began landing on Billy's back as he heard the popping and thumping of other blows crashing onto the backs of his comrades.

Billy closed his eyes and prayed. The beating seemed to go on and on but there was nothing he could do. When it was over the leather straps were untied and the boys were dropped to the ground. Billy fought desperately to get the leather rope from around his thumbs, as there was no feeling in them. He used his teeth until he was finally untied.

Billy looked forward and saw Rattler trying to help Tom Smith. Smith was balled into a fetal position holding onto his side. With his hands free Billy moved up to help Tom. He took his hands and began to untie the leather strips from his thumbs. From the look on his face Billy knew that he was hurt, maybe seriously.

Surrounded by guards the eight boys hobbled back to the barracks with Billy and Rattler helping Tom Smith make his way back.

Once in the barracks they lay Tom in his bunk and tried to help him find a comfortable position. There was none.

Tom looked at Rattler, then back to Billy, while sobbing openly.

"I'm hurt real bad," he said as he pointed to his left side. "It hurts like fire down there. I can't stand it, it hurts so bad."

"Now ya hang on, ya hear me!" Billy said through his own tears. "Ya gonna be alright."

"You boys been good to me, best friends I ever had. I just wish we'd knowed each other without this damn war."

"Now you hush, Tom. Git some rest; we'll stay right with ya 'til ya get better."

Billy and Rattler laid Tom in the best position they could find with Billy lying in the bunk with him. Marcus and Alfred Morgan looked on while John Heatherly tended to his sick brothers.

Tom's pain grew as the day moved into night. By midnight he had developed a fever; then he became chilled. Billy huddled against him trying to stop the chill but he could feel the heat coming from Tom's body. Early the next morning Tom spoke to Billy as the others slept.

"Billy, please tell my maw I'm sorry. Tell her and Paw that I love 'em and miss 'em. Will ya tell 'em that fer me?" Tom said as he sobbed quietly.

"Don't say that, Tom. Ya gonna tell 'em yourself. You hang on now, it'll get better." Billy spoke the words but deep down he feared they were not true.

Tom shivered and groaned, then finally lost consciousness in the early evening. His breathing became short and shallow. Billy tried to give him water but he coughed most of it up. Billy dozed off to sleep early the next morning and his mind slipped into a dream state. He dreamed of the battlefield, the beautiful black stallion, and the strange old man who always appeared in his dreams. When he woke up he struggled to understand but there was only confusion.

Again Billy was trapped in his dream, struggling to free himself until he awoke with a start. When he reached for Tom he felt a body that was cold and lifeless.

Chapter Seventeen

—— OCTOBER 30, 1864 ——

Chicago, Illinois
After Tom Smith's death Billy and Rattler stayed together almost constantly. Small pox swept the camp that fall but neither Billy nor Rattler came down with the disease. Billy was certain that God was finally answering his prayers.

But the Dead House had claimed many others. Aaron and Soloman had both died leaving John as the only survivor of the five Heatherly brothers. John Morgan contracted small pox and died in eleven days. The only good thing about the pox was that it kept the guards away. Small pox made no distinction between the geographic origin of men or the color of their uniform.

Marcus, Billy, Rattler, John Heatherly, and Alfred Morgan huddled around the stove as they contemplated the future.

"I gotta tell ya, Billy, I don't know if we'll survive winter here. It's plum awful, ya gets so cold ya can't feel nothin' and 'em Yankee guards won't lift a toe fer ya," Marcus said.

Billy looked at his brother, then turned to the others. He had never known such agony of the spirit. There was so little hope and the war seemed as if it would go on forever. Deep within the recesses of his mind, the young Confederate's priorities had changed. His only goal was to survive and at Camp Douglas that was an ambitious goal.

"We gotta make it somehow," he said with no real idea as to how they would accomplish that.

"Maybe break free?" Rattler said.

"Ya can't get away with it. It's a thousand miles back south. Ya seen what happened to all them that went out last week. They tunneled out all right but they didn't get far. They're either shot dead or in White Oak Dungeon," John Heatherly told them.

"He's right, ain't no use in tryin' that," Marcus added.

As the North Carolina men contemplated their life in prison a commotion began in the yard. Guards came in yelling and cursing.

"All ya Rebs git yer ass outside; come on, move it," the guards yelled as they herded the Confederates into the prison yard.

Colonel Sweet was waiting to address the prisoners. "As insolent traitors it's understandable that you would be too stupid to conduct yourselves in a proper manner. Therefore I will take it upon myself to see that matters are under control," Sweet told them as if making a picnic announcement. "Because some of you decided to try to escape by tunneling out we will be undertaking a small renovation project. All the barracks will be raised three feet off the ground so the guards can see under them. That should put a stop to the tunnel business." Sweet laughed. "Oh, and one other thing. The escapees hid their crimes under the stoves. Therefore, we shall be removing them all." Sweet started to turn and walk away as men in the ranks began to mumble.

"God have mercy, we'll freeze!" Billy's growing frustration caused him to blurt out the words without forethought.

Sweet turned back to face the prisoners. "Sergeant O'Hara, who said that?"

"That one there," Socks shouted as he moved toward Billy and pulled him out of the ranks.

Sweet walked over to Billy and looked him up and down. "So you don't care for our accommodations?" Sweet said as if it were a serious question. "Gentlemen, escort this young Rebel to White Oak Dungeon. Maybe he'll find it more comfortable there."

"Yes, sir. Move your ass, Reb," Socks shouted as he pulled Billy away.

Billy was taken across the prison yard through two gates, then into a small building at White Oak Square. Once inside the stench was overwhelming. In the dim, unlighted room Billy could see a dark cross-shaped pit about ten feet deep. As he stared at the hole Socks slammed him in the back with his rifle butt, knocking him into the pit. Billy landed on his side where his right hand buried into a small puddle. The stench inside the dungeon itself was nauseating. There were no latrine privileges for occupants of the dungeon.

Billy Long was near his limit. He tried to clean himself as tears slipped from the corners of his eyes. The odor was so bad he thought he might suffocate but there was nothing he could do. He felt his way around as best he could and discovered that one end of the earthen pit was absent of feces.

Billy prayed constantly as the minutes and hours passed. Enough light came through the cracks in the wood so that he could estimate the time of day. He was given bread and water each morning and each evening but there was little comfort as his body began to deteriorate.

He traveled extensively within the confines of his mind, back to Edneyville and to the little Baptist church where he was baptized as a child. He was with Tom Smith again, hiking Bearwallow Mountain, bird hunting and berry picking. He thought of his mother and wept.

"Think only of happy times," he said aloud to himself.

On the fifth day he began to whisper aloud to pass the time. At night the cold was so bad he huddled in the corner of the dark pit with his arms wrapped around himself.

By the eighth day the weather had turned warmer but he had developed the flux, as the men called it. The surgeons called it dysentery. Billy talked aloud now, carrying on conversations with invisible souls who neither heard nor responded. Since there was no response he began to answer for them as if he were an actor playing two parts. The best thing about his little game was that the other party always said what Billy wanted to hear. He marched for hours without moving a step, the exercise having the effect of boosting his spirits.

One day Billy heard two gunshots. He would learn later that O'Hara, Prairie Bill, and Socks had gotten drunk and shot two prisoners on a bet. One man died at the scene; the other died the next day.

Billy could hear hammers banging and boards knocking as the construction on the barracks carried on without him. After his tenth day in the dungeon the hammering stopped.

After two weeks in the solitary pit the guards came to remove him. A small ladder was lowered into the hole and Billy slowly climbed out.

"Well, Reb, how was yer holiday? Yer accommodations were suitable I hope." The guard chuckled.

Once out of the pit Billy could barely walk. They opened the door and pushed him into the sunlight. The brightness blinded him and he fell forward to his knees. The guards came up behind him and one kicked him, shouting and cursing as he prodded him on.

"Git yer ass up, cracker. I'll put ya back in that hole if ya don't git movin'."

Billy climbed to his feet and staggered forward. Slowly he made his way back to barracks number twenty-three. Marcus and Rattler saw him coming and hurried to assist him. The two guards shoved him to the ground then walked away laughing.

Billy looked up at his brother and trusted friend and smiled. His rotting teeth and sunken eyes looked horrible to the others but he was so glad to be out that he didn't notice their expression.

"I been on a holiday," Billy said as he forced a little smile.

Billy looked beyond his brother and his friend at the barracks behind them. "I'll be damned, the barracks is flyin', ain't they?" he commented as he looked at the buildings, which were well above ground.

"Yeah, I reckon so; they're off the ground anyway," Marcus said as he and Rattler picked him up and carried him into the building.

"We got a special treat. It's kind of a reward from all that work we did. Rattler's got somethin' for ya," Marcus said as they laid him in the bunk.

Billy couldn't understand what treat there might have been so he only nodded.

"While ya was gone we had a feast. When we started pulling up the barracks floors we found hundreds of big rats. I mean the biggest damn rats ya ever seen," Marcus said, grinning. "I know a feller'd never think a such, but as it turns out, a rat is pretty good eatin', if I do say so myself."

"Is true. Like chicken," Rattler said, giving Billy water. Billy's condition was serious and his friend knew it.

When Billy was finished with the water, Rattler put down the tin cup and reached for an old ammunition box that had once been used for a seat. He reached down in the box and pulled out a large rat, holding it by the hind legs. The animals front feet and hind feet were tied together. There was a string wound around its head and mouth to prevent it from biting.

"I save for you. Need meat after holiday."

Rattler let his emotions show as a tear trickled down his cheek. The frightful appearance of his friend rocked his stoic demeanor. He held the rat for all to see and Billy smiled in response.

Rattler reached in his pants and pulled his special Cherokee knife from the secret compartment. He pointed the knife at the rat, then spoke to Billy. "Is time to eat. Rat tired of box."

Billy looked at the knife with a strange affection. It seemed that the little token was all that was left of their previous life. He joked with his brother and his Cherokee friend as he watched the preparations.

"That's the biggest damn rat I ever saw," Billy said as he mustered a slight smile.

Sweet had taken their stoves but the prisoners had learned to build small fires on flat pieces of iron the Baptist students brought to them.

The students and some local civilians also smuggled vegetables to the prisoners. Marcus had saved a potato for Billy's homecoming.

"All Yankees ain't bad," Marcus commented as he tapped the edge of the precious iron plate.

Rattler slaughtered the rat while Marcus turned the potato over the little fire. Soon the rat was roasting on a stick.

Billy ate all he could while the others just watched. They roasted the rat's innards, even his head. John Heatherly cracked open the head and ate the cooked brains. Every morsel was devoured until there was nothing but bones.

John Rattler stayed with Billy constantly. Marcus and Rattler brought him extra rations and extra water when they could get them. Slowly Billy began to recover his strength.

Rattler brought extra beans and bread to Billy and he slept on a full stomach for the first time in many months. As he slept through the night his dreams returned. Early in the morning he was awakened with a troubled heart. Something was bothering him but at first he didn't know what. Within a minute or two he understood his own troubled mind and again he was overcome by fear. This time it was a rational fear not vested in dreams.

The disturbance was not imaginary but real, a loud noise, accompanied by cold. It was the winter wind blowing from the north, howling its way across Lake Michigan and ripping through Camp Douglas. This was what his brother and the others had warned him about. Winter in Chicago, they said, was "hell on earth."

Chapter Eighteen

—— NOVEMBER 15, 1864 ——

Chicago, Illinois
The air was cold and the ground frozen as the prisoners filed out of their barracks for another recruiting speech. The Confederates hovered and shivered as Red O'Hara read a recruit announcement from a Union general named Sully.

Sully was on a trip from the western frontier to Camp Douglas for the purpose of recruiting Confederate prisoners for the Union army.

As O'Hara read the announcement some of the men mumbled complaints as they were forced to stand in the cold.

"You will gain your freedom," the announcement proclaimed.

"Yeah, and you Yankee guards will collect a bounty," Edney whispered to those around him. His jaw had healed but he was in no mood to cooperate with his captors.

Billy was cold and sometimes his hunger was beyond tolerance. He looked at Rattler and wondered if anyone else was thinking like he was. He was thinking the unthinkable. Billy was contemplating the possibility of joining the Union army. But when other men stepped forward he stayed where he was. When the traitors were marched away toward freedom and food he jeered at them along with the other prisoners. But deep within the recesses of his mind Billy regretted not going with them.

The men returned to their barracks but the cold was still painful and relentless. The wind blew through the cracks between the wooden planks and under the raised floors. Billy's mind drifted and he considered the possibility of his own death. He began to accept it, nearly to the point of embracing it. If he didn't join the Union army he'd surely die in prison.

The lot of the prisoners was marginally improved due to the Baptist students in the school next to the prison, and God-fearing local citizens who'd come forward to help. Their assistance in the form of extra food and blankets was clearly responsible for saving some men from death.

The citizens of Chicago had also organized to formally protest the inhumane treatment of prisoners at Camp Douglas. They began a letter-writing campaign, complaining to the War Department and to President Lincoln. The protesters had become more active and more vocal as the winter of 1864-65 began. Although some of the citizens involved had Confederate connections most were acting out of humanitarian concern.

The day after the recruiters had taken men away from prison a new group of prisoners arrived. Over the years various escape plots had been conceived or imagined. Rumors of such plots were always circulating. Colonel Sweet would use these perpetual rumors as an excuse to silence his critics. In the wee hours of the morning Colonel Sweet pulled two-thirds of his eight hundred-man guard force off the prison walls and into marching formation.

Under a decree of martial law Sweet marched his men into the city of Chicago and arrested the leaders of the prison protest group. Those who had signed letters or spoken out in public were all arrested. Some of those arrested were very young, some were women, and most were loyal citizens of the United States. One hundred thirty Chicago townspeople were brought to Camp Douglas and thrown in prison along with the Confederates. Colonel Sweet paid Confederate prisoner John T. Shanks to commit perjury against those arrested. Shanks was rewarded for his crimes by way of a captain's commission in the Union army.

Help for the prisoners from the outside was gone. The Confederates and the civilians would have to make it through the winter on their own. That would mean surviving on half rations, no vegetables, and no new blankets. Prospects for C. H. Jordan's undertaker business were very good. He collected $4.87 for every dead Confederate he was supposed to place in a casket and bury. This winter he would add the names of dead civilians to his list of corpses.

Chapter Nineteen

—— DECEMBER 10, 1864 ——

Chicago, Illinois
Billy woke with a start. He was dreaming again, this time he was dreaming about food and warmth. But when he awoke there was only cold and his hunger was stronger than ever. Other men in the barracks were moving about.

Billy started for the door on his way to the latrine. John Edney got up to go with him. As the two stepped into the early morning light a small group of prisoners marched out on detail surrounded by guards. Some of the guards were in front but several more followed from behind.

Patches of snow and ice dotted the prison yard. As the small procession approached Billy Long and Edney, who were headed in the opposite direction, they turned toward the north gate. Red O'Hara was bringing up the rear. When he turned toward the gate he slipped on a patch of ice, which resulted in his feet flying out from under him. O'Hara bounced off the frozen ground once, then came to a rest flat on his back.

Billy stared in disbelief at first not knowing what happened. John Edney took one look at the startled O'Hara and burst out laughing. Within seconds O'Hara was in a sitting position staring at Edney with an angry look. He climbed back to his feet while the other guards took their turns laughing.

Edney and Billy restarted their walk toward the latrine when O'Hara yelled at them to stop.

"Who the hell do ya think ya are, Reb, laughing at me?" O'Hara screamed as he got right up in Edney's face.

"I'm sorry, I didn't mean nothin' by it," Edney said as sincerely as he knew how. He recognized that the situation had become dangerous.

O'Hara turned to the other guards and barked. "Take this Reb bastard to the wall," he shouted as he shifted his rifle from one hand to the other.

Billy tried to speak as two guards came and grabbed Edney by each arm and pulled him away. Billy was frozen by fear. He wanted to do something but he could not think of anything. He tried again to speak but no words came out.

Edney looked back at Billy as the two guards pressed him to the wall, then moved away.

"Now, you Rebel bastard, ain't ya sorry you laughed at Red O'Hara?" the angry guard said as he raised his rifle.

Edney stood erect without expression and he did not speak.

"I'll teach ya Rebs not to laugh at me. Now ya can laugh in hell."

There was a loud bang as a yellow flame accompanied by clouds of smoke came spewing from the muzzle of the rifle. At first Billy hoped that the shot had missed because Edney stood still against the wall with no change of expression. But then his eyes rolled back, closing slowly as his body collapsed in a heap.

"Take his ass to the Dead House. Jordan can haul him off with his next load," O'Hara ordered as he walked away.

Billy Long stood numb and shaken as they took Edney's body away. He turned and leaned against the barracks wall, buried his face in his hands, and sobbed openly. He prayed aloud and asked for forgiveness. He had done nothing to help Edney; he just stood frozen and watched him die. He would never forgive himself, not for the rest of his life.

Chapter Twenty

—— DECEMBER 17, 1864 ——

Chicago, Illinois
Remnants of Confederate General Hood's Army of Tennessee were added to the prison population. The prison was now very overcrowded with the threat of winter hanging over every man.

Rattler and Billy Long had learned to improve their lot by stealing a little extra food and trapping a rat now and then. They stayed together and did little to attract attention from the guards. They were pulled from their barracks for Dead House duty and other chores; otherwise, they had little contact with the men in blue. Men on both sides of the prison's walls spent most of their time hiding from the wrath of winter. Billy's brother Marcus and several other North Carolina men were taken to the overcrowded hospital barracks.

After returning from a trip hauling bodies for undertaker Jordan they discovered that the guards had been drinking while they were away. The prisoners had seen this before and they all recognized that a drunken guard could mean big trouble.

Some of the guards were singing Christmas carols while others hummed along. Billy and Rattler tried not to look in their direction as they headed for their barracks.

"Hey, Rebs, whar ya goin' in such a hurry?" an intoxicated guard shouted at them.

Billy and Rattler continued to walk as if they didn't hear them. "Stop right there, Rebs, or I'll shoot ya in the back!" another guard shouted.

They stopped and slowly turned around to face the intoxicated soldiers. "We're just goin' back to the barracks. We been on Dead House duty," Billy said as he tried to remain calm.

"Come over here, Rebs. We want ya to sing some fer us," the guard said with slurred speech.

Another guard raised his rifle and pointed it at them. "Ya heard the man; now sing."

Billy looked over at Rattler and nodded. He began to sing the only church hymn he could think of at the moment. He tried to smile as the words slowly streamed out in a choppy version of the song he remembered. He elbowed Rattler and urged him on.

"Sing something, damn it," he told Rattler out of the side of his mouth.

Rattler stood motionless, unable to conjure up any words. He did not know any songs other than those of his tribe and they were all in Kituhwa. He couldn't think of anything to sing.

"Why ain't the Injun singin'?" Socks shouted, then took another sip of whisky.

Socks called Rattler closer, then shouted, "I can't hear ya, Injun! Ya ain't singin'!"

Billy rushed up beside Rattler, taking him by the arm. He looked at Rattler, then burst out singing as loud as he could.

Rattler tried to watch Billy and moved his mouth a little but nothing came out.

"This black ass Injun ain't singin'; he's jus' movin' his yap a little," Socks yelled in an angry tone. He reached for Rattler's arm and tried to pull him away. Billy held tight and kept up his singing. He smiled and nodded his head at Socks.

Socks laughed and stumbled in a drunken display as he watched Billy's out-of-tune rendition of the old hymn. Suddenly his laughter shifted back to anger as he turned back to Rattler and grabbed his arm.

"Ya ain't singin', Injun. I reckon I'm gonna have to shoot ya! Ain't that right, boys?" He laughed as the other guards teased him.

"Shoot his ass!" one guard yelled.

"Ya can't hit him. Ya can't shoot shit, much less that damn Injun," another guard chided as they all laughed and jeered.

Socks jerked Rattler away from Billy's grasp then turned to the other guards.

"Take his ass to the wall. I'll show ya who can shoot and who can't."

Two guards came forward and pulled Rattler to the wall. Billy was temporarily consumed by panic but he regained his composure. "Come on now, Socks, ain't no need to shoot him. He ain't no trouble."

Socks was not listening, he was cocking his rifle.

Billy stepped forward and got between Socks and Rattler. "We'll sing some for ya. Whatever ya want. I can sing real good and my Injun friend here'll catch on real quick. Ya just wait and see," Billy said as he tried to force a smile.

Billy took Rattler's arm again and began to sing and shuffle his feet at the same time. The guards watched his little act and laughed out loud. Rattler looked directly at Billy with a tortured expression. Billy could see the fear in his eyes.

"No, no, damn ya. I ain't seen that Injun sing a word. I'm shootin' his ass."

"No, please, don't shoot him," Billy pleaded as two guards took him by the arms and pulled him away again.

Socks raised his rifle as Billy broke free and ran back to stand in front of Rattler.

"Please, oh God, don't shoot! I'm beggin' ya. Please don't shoot." Billy could take no more and he broke down in tears as he begged for his friend's life. Tears poured from his eyes and his words ran together as he begged and cried at the same time.

The guards all burst out laughing. "Shoot the kid first," one guard shouted as the other cheered.

Rattler's face turned stoic as he began to stare into the distance. He raised his head to the sprits and whispered his father's name. The young Cherokee silently asked the spirits to take him home as he lifted his head skyward. "I go home to Snowbird Creek; I am Snowbird," he said as he looked back at Billy.

While pointing and laughing at Billy the guards had become distracted. "I believe that Reb has lost his mind; he's loco," one guard shouted as he witnessed the sad spectacle.

"Yep, I reckon he's plum mad alright. I'm just gonna shoot 'em both," Socks said as he raised his rifle.

Billy raised his arm and shouted again. "Wait! Ya can't shoot now; we were just getting ready to join up with you fellers."

Billy had no idea what caused him to think of such a thing. It was an idea born of desperation. "Yeah, General Sully wants this Injun too. Yes, sir, this here Injun is a tracker, one of the best. Why, I'll bet the general will pay y'all extra for him," Billy said confidently, knowing that the guards were rewarded for bringing in recruits.

Socks lowered his rifle and looked at Billy with a dubious grin. "Ya say ya want to join the Union army?"

"Oh, yes, sir! We been wantin' to real bad. We just didn't get a good chance to do it. Ya know, with all 'em other prisoners around and all." Billy spoke with all the sincerity he could muster, sobbing between phrases. "I'm tellin' ya, this here Injun is the best tracker in the whole Cherokee tribe. General Sully's gonna be real happy when he gets us."

Socks turned back to the other guards as if to seek approval. Then he looked back at the two terrified prisoners. "Alright, Reb, they ain't no backin' down from that. Is ya two willin' to go over right now?"

"Oh, yes, sir! You can sign us up right now! We'll take the oath right now! Why, ya might as well say it. We're Yankees. Yes, sir, by God, we're Yankees. We're the best damn Yankees in the whole army! Just give us the chance and we'll show ya. We're proud to be Yankees! Hooray for ole Abe Lincoln!"

Chapter Twenty-One

—— JANUARY 23, 1864 ——

St. Louis, Missouri

Billy tossed and turned as images danced through his head. He saw images of men jeering and cursing. He saw his brother's emaciated body and images of John Edney dying at the hands of a crazy guard. His mind was filled with conflict and confusion as he dreamed of times past.

Billy and Rattler had been taken to segregated quarters at White Oak Square inside Camp Douglas. A number of defecting prisoners were already there when they arrived. The next morning the cadre of prisoners found themselves standing before Colonel Carroll Potter taking the oath of allegiance to the United States. Within just a few minutes both John Rattler and William Nicholas Long had "swallowed the dog," and joined the Union army. Colonel Potter had been given authority by Generals Pope and Sully to organize the Sixth U.S. Volunteer Infantry. Most of the men for this new regiment would come from behind the prison walls at Camp Douglas.

The new recruits were fed and dressed in new blue uniforms at Camp Frye, which was located just a few miles from the prison. After a two-day stay at Frye they were loaded on train cars and taken south, where they were ferried down river to St. Louis, Missouri.

Billy's restless night came to an end when he awoke to another cold winter morning. He and the other new recruits had been called "Galvanized Yankees" by Colonel Potter, a term used to describe a prisoner's change of allegiance. At St. Louis they were organized into companies and loaded onto a riverboat called the *Effie Deans*. The men were closely guarded and kept to quarters the entire way, yet a number of the former prisoners had taken advantage of the many opportunities to escape. Billy was of no mind to try it and Rattler had sworn his loyalty and companionship to the teenager who'd saved his life. They planned to stay.

One of Colonel Potter's first objectives was to get the new Galvanized Yankees into better physical condition. Many of the prisoners at Camp Douglas were suffering from various maladies. Some of the men had lost one-third of their body weight or more and most suffered from some level of dysentery. The new recruits were being fed very well and Billy could see the difference in Rattler almost immediately.

Billy awoke to find Rattler staring over the rails at the opposite bank. Rattler turned and smiled as his friend came to stand beside him.

"*Sho*, my Cheokee friend," Billy said with a big smile.

"*Sho*," Rattler responded with an equal smile.

Billy put his hand on Rattler's shoulder as they both stood at the rail and gazed at their surroundings.

"Better ride boat, no iron machine," Rattler said, reminding Billy of his distrust of trains.

"I don't care what we ride as long as they keep feedin' us. I never had so much beef in my whole life," Billy said shaking his head in disbelief.

Rattler's head bowed and a worried look crossed his face. "You save my life. I stay with you always, you spirit brother," Rattler said.

"It's alright, my Injun brother. We're out of that damn prison, ain't we?" Billy said with a broad grin.

Worry still dominated Rattler's expression. He seemed troubled.

"Why you no worry? Me worry Yankees take me away, no be with you."

Billy smiled broadly and put his arm around his friend's shoulders and tugged firmly.

CHAPTER TWENTY-ONE

"Hey, my friend, I got that one figured out. I think we can stay together as long as we want," Billy said confidently. "Just so we don't run into no smart ass Yankee who speaks Cherokee."

Rattler looked at his friend with a confused expression. "Colonel say we all go different place maybe," Rattler said.

"Here's how we do it," Billy said as he glanced in both directions to make sure no one was listening. "You're a tracker, ain't ya?"

"All Cherokee man learn to track. I man, I track, so? Rattler replied.

"Well, here's how it is. When I first met ya back in Asheville the one thing I saw right off is how ya don't never say nothin' about much. Now in this here situation that's a good thing. Ain't none of these Yankees heard you say hardly a word," Billy said laughing slightly.

"So here's the way it is from now on. The reason ya ain't sayin' much is because ya don't speak no English. I'm your interpreter, so we got to stay together. Otherwise, them Yankees will miss out on the best tracker in the whole world." Billy burst out laughing when he finished revealing his plan.

Rattler smiled but he still looked confused. "Me no understand. You no speak Kituhwa," he said with his worried expression returning.

Billy laughed again. "I know that. You know that. But them damn Yankees don't know it. You just say whatever you wanna say. I'll make some sounds back to ya, then I'll turn around and tell them Yankees whatever they want to hear."

Rattler considered the plan and decided he liked it. "No like talk no how. This good. I only talk to you, my brother." Rattler nodded as a big smile spread across his face.

"Chumba reaka theump!" Billy said as he instantly conjured up some sounds.

"What?" Rattler asked, as he was initially confused at Billy's mumbling.

"Damn, Injun! Don't ya speak no Cherokee?" Billy slapped him on the back repeatedly, laughing as he talked. "I don't know what I just said, but it means 'let's go eat some more.'"

The two inseparable friends started for the food line.

PART THREE

Chapter Twenty-Two

—— FEBRUARY 12, 1865 ——

Fort Leavenworth, Kansas
Billy Long and John Rattler found themselves assigned to Company H of the Sixth U.S. Volunteer Infantry. Their company was commanded by a twenty-year-old, Lieutenant Paul York from Springfield, Massachusetts. Most of the other regular soldiers were from Georgia and Alabama.

York was over six feet tall with a slender build. His blond hair was thin and straight hanging just over his ears. The young lieutenant had bright blue eyes that conveyed a vibrant personality and a jovial wit. Having recently come from civilian life, he held none of the hard feelings associated with war veterans who had seen their friends die in battle. The Galvanized Yankees were a mere curiosity to him.

Billy considered it good fortune to be assigned to York. Out of six full regiments of Galvanized Yankees none of the Confederate prisoners was allowed to be an officer with one exception—John Shanks. Shanks had been on Colonel Sweet's payroll as a spy and traitor against the other prisoners at Camp Douglas. Shanks committed perjury for Colonel Sweet and the officer's commission was part of the payoff. He was also the principal witness in Sweet's fraudulent case against Chicago's civilians. Billy Long did not want to be anywhere near him, and none of the converted Confederates wanted to be assigned to him.

Rattler had just turned eighteen and Billy was still seventeen. Lieutenant York did his duty and expected the same from his men. To the two mountain boys from western North Carolina York didn't seem to be a "kid," but to some of the older men he was. York soon learned that the young mountaineer and his Cherokee friend could be depended on to get things done.

Some regular army units were mustering out of service in the area. Post assignments and duty that had been the responsibility of the regulars was transferred to the U.S. Volunteer regiments. Within just a few days after their arrival at Fort Leavenworth Billy and Rattler received their first assignment as soldiers in the United States Army.

Lieutenant York called his men to formation and selected twenty soldiers to accompany a supply train to Fort Kearney. They would also be responsible for carrying the mail going west. In the summertime the trip wasn't too bad, but in February it could be very dangerous. Sudden storms on the plains had taken many to their graves. When York and his men departed the weather was mild.

Billy Long and John Rattler were among the twenty selected for escort duty to Fort Kearney.

"Private Long, can your Cherokee friend find his way if the weather turns bad?" York asked.

Billy turned to Rattler and mumbled a series of phrases and sounds composed of nothing but complete gibberish.

Rattler looked back at Billy and responded in Kituhwa. Billy had no idea what Rattler said but after listening for a few seconds her turned back to York.

"Yes, sir! He said he can find his way in the snow," Billy told him confidently.

"Good. All right, men, draw your rations and be ready to leave first thing tomorrow morning. You will take nothing with you except what is absolutely necessary," York told them.

When York dismissed his men Rattler and Billy returned to the barracks and began their preparations.

"What did you say to me back there?" Billy asked Rattler.

Rattler looked back at Billy and smiled. "I say you speak pig droppings and you crazy."

Billy and Rattler laughed and continued their preparations.

"Duh, moo kam sam," Billy said to Rattler with a big smile on his face.

"What?" Rattler said, not sure what to make of Billy's babbling.

"That means you're full of pig droppings yourself. Don't you understand no Cherokee?"

Both men burst out laughing.

When Billy and Rattler came to formation the next morning the wagons were already in place for the trip west. All the army guards were given carbines and sixty rounds of ammunition. Civilian teamsters drove the wagons and handled the freight. The army's responsibility was to protect the wagon train and guide it safely to Fort Kearney.

"Hey, Private Long. I want you and Rattler out front. Tell Rattler to make sure we stay on the right trail," York commanded.

"Yes, sir!" Billy said.

Billy and Rattler trotted to the front and moved out approximately fifty yards in front of the wagon train.

"Rummy tum tum, toot ta toot," Billy said to Rattler grinning.

Rattler shook his head and chuckled. "What that mean? I think, no want to know."

"That's Indian for 'don't ya get our ass lost,'" Billy said with a laugh.

"No kidding, Rattler, I'm a little worried. Can you get us there? That lieutenant really thinks you're a tracker. We aint' never seen country like this."

"I track; you no worry. I get us there," Rattler said.

Nights on the trail were chilly and uncomfortable. Camp time was spent preparing meals and keeping warm. The threat of winter weather kept all at bay including hostile tribes in the area. There was little excitement, only the drudgery of daily travel and cold camp life.

Twenty days later the party topped a hill with Rattler and Billy out front. Billy turned and ran back to Lieutenant York, who was with the lead wagon on horseback. "There she is!" Billy yelled as he pointed in the direction of the fort.

York rode forward at a gallop passing Billy as he went to the top of the hill where Rattler stood waiting. Rattler pointed to the west where Fort Kearney could be seen with the naked eye.

Billy ran and eventually caught up with the young lieutenant. "I told ya, by God!" Billy said, gasping for breath. "He's the best damn tracker in the whole Cherokee nation." Billy was trying to hide his own amazement.

York looked into the distance, then turned to the two teenagers. "Great job, men. Now let's get this train into the fort."

Lieutenant York had delivered the wagon train without any loss of men or supplies. For the young officer it was his first successful assignment.

The men were assigned barracks and given hot food and coffee. Rattler and Billy hovered around a stove in the barracks and drank their coffee while celebrating their success. "Damn, you are a tracker, ain't ya?" Billy said.

Rattler turned to Billy and laughed. He looked at him as if he were an idiot and spoke in Kituhwa.

"What the hell did you just say?" Billy said as he realized Rattler was ridiculing him.

"I say, 'easy.' Blind dog find fort," Rattler said with a smile.

"I don't get it. What's so funny?" Billy asked wanting to understand the humor.

"I follow telegraph poles. Soldier wire go fort to fort."

———

CHAPTER TWENTY-TWO

That evening Billy sought out Lieutenant York finding him in the sutler's store. "Lieutenant, sir, could I ask you a question?"

"Sure, Private Long, what's on your mind?"

"I was wonderin' if you were good with letters. I'd like to write home to my family in North Carolina. When we were at the Camp Douglas prison we weren't allowed to write nobody. They don't know if I'm alive or dead," Billy said, a forlorn look on his face.

"I'm not great at writing but I can get by," the young officer responded.

"I can write some but not too good. I was wondering if you'd help me?" Billy said.

"Sure, I can do that. We've got plenty of time here until the army tells us where to go next."

Dearest Family,

I got captured at Camp Vance. They sent us to prison and life there was hell. They was starving us to death and men froze almost every night. Guards would torture us and shoot people for no kinda reason.

I rekon Paw will be mad at me but I had to git out of that prison fer I'd been dead by now. The Yankees told us we could com out west and fight the Injuns. They promised we'd never have to fight our folks. I had to do it. I joined the Yankee army. I'm hopin to com home when my year is done.

I eat good now and my strength has com back to me.

I pray to God that the war will be over and we'll all be together again. God bless.

Your lovin son,
Billy Long

Chapter Twenty-Three

—— MARCH 10, 1865 ——

Fort Kearney, Nebraska Territory
A winter storm passed over the Great Plains bringing a halt to the activities of both soldier and native. High winds and deep drifts prevented even the hardiest of man or beast from traveling. Billy and the small detachment of men from Company H found themselves confined to quarters both day and night. Their only duty was to keep the fires going.

Some of the men had taken to drink. Rattler wouldn't even smell it but Billy tried it. The rye whiskey tasted so bad that Billy decided Rattler had the correct opinion on the matter.

"Whiskey no good for Snowbird. Bad spirit in bottle," Rattler told Billy.

"I don't know about the spirits, but the stuff tastes plum awful."

Lieutenant York began to spend more and more time with Billy and Rattler. They played marbles on the barracks floor. York taught Billy and Rattler how to play card games. York and Billy talked of home and girls while Rattler listened and whittled sticks with his ornate Cherokee knife.

Within three weeks of the paralyzing storm the weather turned warm and the snow began to melt. The men at the fort were all anxious to escape the boredom and confinement that had been their lot for weeks.

The whiskey was gone and food supplies were running low. All of the men including Lieutenant York expected to be returning to Fort Leavenworth as soon as the weather improved.

Billy and York were in the sutler's store when a corporal came to York and told him he was to report to the commanding officer at once. Billy wondered what the urgency was, but within a few minutes he thought little of it.

It was over an hour later when York returned to the barracks seeking out Billy and Rattler.

"Men we just got orders to move tomorrow morning," York said with a firm voice.

"Hallelujah, I'll be glad to get out of this mud hole," Billy announced before he had heard all York had to say.

"We're not going back to back Fort Leavenworth," York said in a solemn tone. "We have orders from Colonel Potter. Back in January a party of Cheyenne Indians raided a ranch operated by William Morris and his family.

"There were four men, two children, and this Morris fellow's wife. Some trappers got word back to Colonel Potter. They found the men all dead along with one of the children. Sarah Morris and her infant are missing. It's believed they were taken by the Cheyenne." York paused when he said this; even the most inexperienced men in the company could conjure up the ramifications of that statement.

"Colonel says we're going after them. We're going with an Iowa Cavalry company and we'll be getting mounts."

"I ain't rode a horse since I left home," Billy told Rattler.

"Need horse, good spirit. Bad horse, bad ride," Rattler said.

"The colonel picked us to go on account of you, Rattler. He expects you to track down that raiding party," the lieutenant said. "The Iowa boys are expected here tonight. We'll be leaving tomorrow morning headed west following the Platte." Then the young officer dismissed his men.

As soon as they were alone Billy grabbed Rattler, turning him around.

CHAPTER TWENTY-THREE

"Oh shit, Rattler, this is serious. We're in big trouble," Billy told him, almost screeching as he said it.

"No big worry," the Cherokee responded.

"No big worry! Damn, there's a woman and a baby out there somewhere. It's thousands of square miles and there's a bunch of mean Indians between here and there. I don't guess they'd take kindly to givin' up that woman even if we did stumble across 'em somehow, wanderin' around in the middle of nowhere. Believe me, if something goes wrong, somebody will hang for it!" Billy said in a near panic.

Rattler stared forward without acknowledging the lecture.

"Not to mention that our lead scout is an eighteen-year-old Cherokee working in a foreign land, who ain't never tracked nothin' but telegraph poles." Billy sat down and buried his face in his hands. "Oh, God! We're goin' back to prison. No, hell, worse. They're gonna shoot us."

John Rattler stared straight ahead and said nothing. He reached inside his uniform and pulled out his beautiful Cherokee knife. He rolled it in his hands, then looked west, into the distance. "How any man track?" he calmly asked Billy.

Billy looked at Rattler in frustration. "I have no idea; that's the problem! Ya ain't got much of an idea yourself."

John Rattler picked up a stick and began to slide the knife blade slowly off the tip of the stick, peeling thin layers of wood with each stroke. He turned and looked directly at Billy. "He follow tracks."

Chapter Twenty-Four

—— MARCH 18, 1865 ——

North of the Platte River, Nebraska Territory
Lieutenant Waightsill Wright of the Third Iowa Cavalry was senior to Lieutenant York. Wright, in command as Company B of the Third Iowa Cavalry and Company H of the Sixth U.S. Volunteers, followed Private John Rattler and Private Billy Long out onto the great plain. Billy was feeling much better about it. He learned that the search's starting point was at the Morris Ranch. The ranch was right on the river. All they had to do was take the flatboat ferry to the north shore and follow their way along the north bank of the Platte.

Although cooler air prevailed the days were sunny and bright. Many parts of the vast grassland were free of snow and ice. The river ran cold and high on the bank as it rounded the bends. The men looked into the distance and saw a vast heard of buffalo on the move north in search of early spring grass. A party of sixty-four U.S. mounted soldiers followed the Platte River heading west.

Billy and Rattler rode a quarter mile ahead along with two Iowa boys. Billy's riding was questionable but he was a quick learner and he got a good horse. They'd been following the river and riding hard for three and a half days when Rattler first pointed out a spot in the distance the others didn't see it. Then one by one they saw it.

The four young soldiers took off at a gallop toward the site. When they got to the ranch there were only remains. The ranch house lay in a pile of black ashes and there were mounds in the earth where the victims' bodies had been buried. The only hope for the woman and her baby was to somehow pick up the raiding party's trail here.

Billy and the Iowans rode back to inform the officers while Rattler rode around the ranch. He found tracks coming in and out of the area in several places. But when he reached a point northwest of the ranch he picked up an old trail heading due north. Rattler rode back and forth very slowly. Rattler's sharp eyes picked up antelope tracks crossing the rider's main path. As he looked over the area he realized that there must be over one hundred riders in the party. Tracks could be seen going in both directions, north and south. Rattler knew that they had come to the ranch the same way they left.

When the main body of soldiers arrived at the ranch Billy rode over to Rattler, presumably for the purpose of translating the Cherokee tracker's words.

Billy and Rattler rode over to the officer and Billy made his report. "Sir, we found the trail of the Cheyenne but there's somethin' ya need to know. Private Rattler says there's more than a hundred riders."

"That makes no difference; we've got repeating carbines and pistols. They'll not stand up to us," Lieutenant Wright pronounced.

They pushed hard, moving from sunup to sundown, following the trail for three days. The young lieutenant was determined to succeed at his mission.

On the fourth day they met a trapper with two native women traveling with him. They had crossed the path of the Cheyenne party while making their way south. The trapper knew the location of their camp and he told Rattler and Billy how to find the creek leading to them. His most important information beside the camp location was that he had seen a white woman with them.

"Ya just take up that creek and ya follers it yonder 'til ya gits near the headwaters. You'll find 'em Injuns thar. I wouldn't be a hankerin' too hard to fine 'em if I was you. They's more'n a hundred braves thar."

Billy looked at Rattler and swallowed hard. "Ya know, I ain't never been in a real fight. Never had a chance," Billy said as he turned and looked north. He was thinking of the war in the east and his early capture.

Rattler looked back at the two young lieutenants coming up fast.

"You get chance soon."

Billy reported to the officers who ordered them on.

The farther they went the more tracks they found. Some coming, some going. Now some of the tracks were fresh, unlike what they'd seen at the ranch. Soon they reached an intersection in the trails. The ground was choppy and broken indicating a lot of recent activity.

"We're close," Rattler said as he climbed back on his horse.

Billy's palms began to sweat and his thirst seemed to overwhelm him. "John Rattler! Whatever happens don't let them take me. Shoot me if you have to but don't let them take me alive."

Rattler laughed at Billy's fear. "Braves no want you. No worry, they kill you."

"No, damn it. It ain't funny. Ya know what they'll do to a white man," Billy said in an obvious state of stress.

They moved slower now, carefully studying each subtle rise in the ground. Billy expected to sight the camp or hostiles any minute.

Early on the morning of April 1, 1865, they awoke to visitors in the camp. An elderly Pawnee woman with an Indian boy of about twelve years of age calmly walked toward the soldiers accompanied by a white woman. The woman was Sarah Morris.

The Cheyenne had broken camp and left because they knew the soldiers were coming. They freed Mrs. Morris and left the old lady to return with her and the Pawnee boy.

Sarah Morris ran to the men in tears. "They killed my husband. One of them stomped my baby and she died."

She fell to her knees and cried while the two Iowa boys and the two mountaineers stood stunned for a brief moment before rushing to help her up. Lieutenant Wright and Lieutenant York came to meet her and soon the whole camp surrounded the little group.

"How long have they been gone?" Wright asked.

Billy could tell that Wright intended to follow them if possible.

After a few minutes of trying to understand the old Pawnee woman Sarah Morris told them what they needed to know. "It's been three days."

"They are long gone from here," York told Lieutenant Wright.

"Yeah, and we've got what they sent us after," Wright added.

Within the hour the party was turned around, headed south.

Chapter Twenty-Five

—— APRIL 12, 1865 ——

Fort Kearney, Nebraska Territory
The return trip was slower due to the civilians riding packhorses and the lack of urgency. Rattler and Billy rode out front enjoying their role as scouts.

Late in the afternoon the soldiers boarded the flatboat and crossed to the south side of the Platte. As they rode on with the sight of Fort Kearney growing closer they heard gunfire. Billy rode back to the officers while Rattler galloped toward the fort to investigate further.

Lieutenant Wright listened to the report of gunfire along with Lieutenant York. More shots were heard. "Leave one man with the civilians," Wright shouted.

Lieutenant York's horse spun around as York listened to the senior officer.

"You take your men and form them out to the right!" Wright called to York.

"Sergeant! Move some of your men off to that side trail over there," the officer shouted as he pointed.

Billy rode back toward the fort searching for Rattler while Wright waited for all his men to get into position.

"Lock and load your weapons!" Wright shouted. The order was repeated up and down the line.

"Lock and load!"

Wright raised his hand and signaled them forward at a slow trot.

Billy searched frantically for Rattler. He could see that the Cherokee had covered a substantial part of the distance between them and the fort. He found Rattler riding back toward him. The two men had pulled their horses to a stop when Billy realized that Rattler was smiling.

"What is that grin all about?" Billy said with his adrenalin pumping and his heart pounding.

"No see fight."

"What? What is the shooting about?" Billy asked.

"Gate open. People outside, shoot guns. No fight," Rattler told him.

Billy shook his head in a state of obvious confusion. "Are they practice shooting?"

"No think so. Think soldiers drunk. See men dance," Rattler said.

Billy turned and rode back toward Lieutenant Wright and the approaching soldiers. He waved his hat bringing the entire formation to a halt.

"Sir, ya ain't gonna believe this but Rattler says he went up closer and it looks like the men at the fort are drunk, or gone loco or something." Billy saw Wright's confused expression change to one of annoyance.

More gunshots were popping in the distance.

"You better not lead us into an ambush," Wright said in a threatening tone.

"There's still shooting going on down there! You do hear the gunfire, don't you, Private?" the lieutenant asked.

Before Billy could respond two riders were spotted on their way out to meet them. Lieutenants Wright and York moved out front and rode along with Billy and Rattler directly behind them. As they moved closer to the fort the riders could be heard shouting and whooping as they came. For a moment the officers thought the commotion was caused by their own triumphant return. They were close enough now to see men at the fort shooting guns into the air.

The approaching riders closed the distance and rode up to the officers waving their hats. "Bobby Lee surrendered!" one of them shouted.

"The war is over! Hallelujah, praise God! Whoopee!" the other man screamed.

Wright and York looked at each other and simultaneously threw off their hats turning toward their men.

"Lee surrendered!" Wright shouted.

The Iowa boys went into screaming fits with York joining in. But the men of Company H, Sixth U.S. Volunteer Infantry just sat in their saddles and stared at each other quietly. Many had served under Lee and understood something the Iowa boys couldn't understand. To men from the South, even the ones who'd gone over to the Union side, Robert E. Lee was a man above all others. Lee walked this earth as a mortal but to them he represented something much greater.

Chapter Twenty-Six

—— APRIL 20, 1865 ——

Fort Kearney, Nebraska Territory
Things at the fort had settled down as the celebration had been severely muted by the news of President Lincoln's assassination. The sad news came in over the wire only a few days after word of Lee's surrender.

Men stayed near the telegraph to hear the latest news from the east. Most of the whiskey supplies had been consumed but Rattler and Billy didn't drink a drop. The soldiers were expecting supplies from Fort Leavenworth at any time. Many of them also knew that they would be mustering out of the army soon.

Billy and Rattler spent a good deal of time with Lieutenant York. He participated in the drinking the first night but had since joined his two young friends as a nondrinker.

"Ya know, York, I'm real glad we joined up and became Galvanized Yankees," Billy said as he contemplated his future. "When I get back home I hope we can help bring the country back together. My year'll be up in December. I can't wait to see my folks. Billy sipped his coffee. "Today's my eighteenth birthday. But it just seems like any other day out here."

York put his arm on Billy's shoulder and looked at Rattler. "Colonel

Potter all the way up to General Sully and General Pope know about us saving that Morris lady. Every soldier in the West has heard about the Cherokee tracker. The war is over and we're heroes. It can't get much better than that! Happy birthday, Billy."

"I guess I'm having the best birthday I could expect," Billy said.

"I also have some news for you two. I got a telegram from Colonel Potter last night. We'll be stationed here for another month or so; then we'll be moving out," York said calmly.

"Where we goin'?" Billy asked.

"We're being posted at Camp Douglas," York responded.

Billy jumped up from his seat. "What?" Billy almost screamed. "I ain't goin' back to that hell! I just can't."

York laughed but neither Billy nor Rattler caught onto the joke. "It's Camp Douglas in the Utah Territory; it's a stop on the Overland Stage route," York told them. "We're going west."

Some of the men and several civilians gathered in front of the barracks watching as the supply wagons came in from Fort Leavenworth. Members of the Fifth Wisconsin Cavalry escorted the wagons. The Iowa boys were being replaced and they would be returning to Leavenworth for mustering out.

York, Billy, and Rattler watched and listened as the Iowa boys talked of their wives and sweethearts and the prospect of going home.

The mail would be carried back on the return trip, so Billy asked York to help him write another letter to his family. He still had no word from them, nor any indication of what happened to his brother Marcus at Camp Douglas, Illinois.

Dearest Family,
I write you cause so much has changed since I wrote you last. I am amongst Indian country but by the grace of God I've seen no fightin.

News of General Lee's surrender reached here not long ago. Many of us southern boys ain't happy by it but we're all glad the war is done fer. I rekon all are saddened by Mr. Lincoln's death.

My army time will be done in December. I will be so happy cause I want to com home somethin awful.

Have you news of Marcus? I worry of him somthin fierce.
Billy

Chapter Twenty-Seven

—— JUNE 30, 1865 ——

Fort Kearney, Nebraska Territory
York's detachment of Company H, Sixth U.S. Volunteers left early in the morning light and headed west on the Overland Stage route. They were joined by a detachment of the Eighteenth Infantry regular army troops also on their way to Utah. Both detachments expected Rattler and Billy to guide them there.

The Kearney stage station was just west of the fort. York and his men rode to the station along with the regulars, where they met the party to be escorted all the way to Salt Lake City.

When they got to the station they found several civilians including a newspaper reporter from the East. The civilians would be traveling in a bright red Concord stagecoach. These beautiful New Hampshire-made coaches were the finest of the day. Besides their distinctive red color the coaches featured sidelights and interior candle lamps. Leather curtains were fitted to keep out rain and dust, although not very successfully. The large boot in the rear carried ordinary baggage and mail sacks. Each passenger was allowed twenty-five pounds of free luggage but they paid extra for any overage. Passengers could ride side by side on three seats, holding up to nine people inside. More passengers could ride on top of the coach. The fare from Atchison to California was four hundred fifty dollars, a small fortune in 1865.

As the procession moved out Billy was taken by the striking appearance of formation. The bright blue uniforms of the soldiers contrasted with the bright red coach. The early morning sun rose behind them as they headed out onto the plain.

Billy was beginning to feel proud as he and Rattler rode out in front of the stagecoach and the other soldiers.

"Find trail easy," Rattler said to Billy as they rode along. "Many men pass here, leave many sign."

It took four and a half days to reach Fort McPherson, then four more to Julesburg where Fort Sedgwick marked a fork in the trail. Billy and Rattler then led the party on to Camp Collins, Colorado, which took another nine days.

Billy and Rattler spent evenings exploring with Lieutenant York. All three young men marveled at the spectacular scenery that met them at most every turn. The three had become the closest of friends. York soon admitted that he knew Rattler not only spoke English, he also understood. York only laughed and ordered them not to tell anyone else.

There were reports of hostile Indians but their party met only friendly natives. Wild game was abundant and the weather was moderate most of the time. They roasted fresh meat almost every night.

The young soldiers met travelers coming east including a detachment from the Eleventh Ohio Cavalry headed east for mustering out. There were Galvanized Yankees among the members of the Ohio regiment. When they camped together at Collins, boys from the Carolinas, Georgia, and Alabama traded stories with each other. Some had not heard from their families in a year of two. Some had mixed feelings about the war, but to a man they were glad it was over.

It took two more weeks to cross the high country of the Wasatch Range and reach Fort Bridger. There were reports of Sioux warriors to the north. Billy and Rattler stayed alert but they were never threatened.

CHAPTER TWENTY-SEVEN

On July 8, 1865, the detachment of the Sixth U.S. Volunteers and the rest of the party began their final march toward Camp Douglas. Even though the post was hundreds of miles away from the other Camp Douglas in Illinois, the ex-Confederates didn't like going there just because of the name.

When they arrived they were totally shocked by what awaited them. They found a beautiful post, occupied by California and Nevada cavalry soldiers. The Westerners were glad to have these Galvanized Yankees because the arrival of the replacements meant that they could all go home.

The riders were expecting to find the same dreary conditions that existed at other posts in the West. But this Camp Douglas was the antithesis of the Camp Douglas that they had escaped by "swallowing the dog."

The streets were wide and attractive. The main streets were planked. They rode into the fort with the entire garrison standing in review while a brass band played marching music. The California and Nevada men welcomed the ex-Confederates as if the war had never happened.

There were neatly arranged buildings made of frame lumber and stone with grass growing in front. The wooden posts and trim were all painted white. The interiors of the barracks were neat and attractive. The accommodations were more like what one would find in most hotels of the day. There were real beds with real cotton sheets.

Camp Douglas was positioned on a high hill overlooking Salt Lake City. The views in every direction were beautiful. There was plenty of clean water and forage was plentiful. Billy and the others couldn't believe their good fortune.

This was their new home and they were to be there until further notice. These mountain boys from western North Carolina would be protecting the mail and the telegraph line and escorting coaches to and from Sacramento and San Francisco.

Chapter Twenty-Eight

—— SEPTEMBER 17, 1865 ——

Camp Douglas, Utah Territory
Lieutenant York and his two trackers became widely known throughout the territory. They had tracked Indians, outlaws, and livestock all to the delight of the civilians. The three young men worked together, traveled together, and lived together. All of them practiced their marksmanship in a competition with each other. All three had become experts with both a rifle and pistol. Rattler could shoot small targets tossed into the air.

They joked and teased about the fact that none of these frontier veterans had ever been in any kind of battle. Unlike most of the other soldiers they stayed away from the bottle.

Lieutenant York was returning from Salt Lake City approaching Camp Douglas when he heard a gunshot. As he got closer a rider came out to meet him.

"Sir, ya better come quick before Private Long hurts somebody," the messenger said with some urgency.

"Private Billy Long?" York asked.

"Yes, sir, Private Billy Long. He's mighty drunk," the soldier told him.

York kicked his horse into a gallop and headed over the last stretch of land between him and the camp. When he got to the barracks he found

John Rattler halfway up a ladder that was leaned against the barracks roof. There were many other soldiers gathered at the site. On top of the roof he saw Billy Long with no shirt on and barefoot, a half-empty bottle of rye in one hand and waving a pistol in the other.

"Don't ya come up that damn ladder! I'll shoot your ass," Billy said as his words twisted into a slurred mumble.

"I'm gonna shoot somebody!" Billy screamed as he took another huge gulp of the brown whiskey.

Rattler turned to York and shook his head. "I don't know. Come back find Billy drunk," Rattler said as he stopped cautiously at the top of the ladder.

"Billy, come down from there," York shouted up to him.

"I ain't goin' no damn where. I'm holding on. I ain't afraid to fight!" Billy said as he waved the pistol around in the air. "I wanna fight some goddamn Yankees!"

When the drunken soldier waved the pistol around a second time the gun went off. Fortunately it was pointed skyward at the time and no one was hurt, at least not from the gunshot. The force from the .44-caliber revolver kick hit Billy's hand just as he was leaning backwards. He fell onto the roof dropping the pistol and breaking the whiskey bottle.

He lay limp for a second or two, then rolled off the backside of the roof plopping like a wet rag into the dirt in back of the barracks. Rattler hurried down the ladder and several others ran around one end of the barracks while York went the other way. They found William Nicholas Long lying face down and unconscious. He had a small cut on his face but otherwise he seemed remarkably unhurt.

"Billy? Billy, are you all right?" York asked as two men took his arms and tried to stand him up.

"Go ahead and shoot me, I ain't nothin' but a coward," Billy said in a half conscious state. "Shoot me, damn it! Just shoot me."

"You hush, Billy. We gotta get you to bed before somebody finds out about this," York said as he signaled for the men to carry him toward the barracks door. "Does anybody know what the hell happened here?"

CHAPTER TWENTY-EIGHT

Billy was unconscious now but he continued to mumble incoherently. Occasionally he sobbed out loud. As they brought him through the door he began to throw up.

"Damn," York said as some of the disgusting bile splattered onto his polished boots. "Get a bucket!"

Rattler got a wet rag and wiped off Billy's face as they laid his limp body on the bed.

"No wonder he's sick," one of the men said as he pointed to the little field table beside the bed. There were two whiskey bottles sitting empty in the middle of the table.

York looked at the bottles. "It's a damn good thing he puked or he might have died from that much whiskey."

"All right, you men go on now, leave him alone. Private Rattler will stay with him. The show's over."

As he got up to leave York noticed two folded pieces of paper and a torn envelope sitting on the little table. "Rattler, was there a mail call while I was gone?"

"Mail come, yes," Rattler responded.

York picked up the two pages and read silently.

Edneyville, North Carolina
July 1, 1865

Dear Private Long,
We got yer ledder that you wrote us from Kanzaes. After you lef your brother at prison he died not long after. James was killed trin to sav Atlanter.

Yer Maw was plum sic on account of Marcus an James a dyin. She caught croop and died. The Yankees com thru her a robbin and steelin. They don unspeakable things to our womenfolk.

No, I ain't got four sons no more. They is all dead ceptin' little John and my girls. You ain't got no family her.

Ain't no Tories or traitors welcome her. You ain't never welcome her again. Don't you never com back her.
Edneyville, Mr. W Long
North Carolina

The last of the Galvanized Yankees reported to Fort Leavenworth for mustering out. Some men went back home to the South; others stayed in the West, and a very few joined the regular army.

When the roster of men mustering out of the army from Company H, Sixth U.S. Volunteer Infantry were presented to the U.S. Army provost the names of William Nicholas Long and John Rattler were not on the list. They remained in the West as members of the regular army.

Chapter Twenty-Nine

—— NOVEMBER 11, 1872 ——

Fort Klamath, Oregon
Lieutenant Paul York led his small detachment of scouts from Fort Klamath, Oregon, toward the California border. Riding beside him were Billy Long and John Rattler. The formation was traveling west on the way to Crescent City, California, to meet a party of civilians. The dignitaries would be arriving by sea. The scout's mission was to escort the civilians from the coast to the army camp at Yreka, California. Lieutenant Colonel Frank Wheaton, the fort commander, indicated these were very high-level civilians traveling under special protection from the War Department in Washington, D.C.

Billy Long was now twenty-five years old. He had become a good soldier and a good tracker thanks to the teachings of his Cherokee friend. He once made corporal but was busted back to private after being jailed for drunkenness and disorderly conduct. The young scout stayed too long in a San Francisco bar. Long had overheard a conversation between two other drinking soldiers. One man was boasting of the Rebels he'd killed and the role he'd played in "torching" Atlanta at the end of the Civil War. Billy started an argument, called the man a liar, then punched him in the face.

Lieutenant York and John Rattler went to the San Francisco jail and posted bail for Billy. The punishment from the army could have been much worse but York was able to intervene on his behalf.

Rattler followed Billy whenever he could and did his best to keep him out of trouble when he was drinking. Billy was threatened by his growing attraction to whiskey and both York and Rattler knew it. Rattler had carried Billy out of many bars and saloons in the Northwest Territory. He would nurse Billy back to a sober condition only to have the same thing happen again in a week or a month.

"Hey, Yorkie, how much time we gonna have in Crescent City?" Billy asked.

"We're supposed to stay until our fancy guests arrive. I don't know exactly," York said.

"Maybe they'll be a while and we can enjoy a little nightlife in town."

"Don't you go getting yourself in any more trouble. Me and Rattler are tired of tracking you. Your tracks sometimes lead to jail," York said.

"I ain't gonna do nothin' 'cept enjoy a little company with the fine ladies in town," Billy responded.

The men arrived at the headquarters of Colonel Alvan C. Gillem. Gillem had established an army post at Fairchild Ranch near Dorris, California, in order to be closer to the current Indian trouble. Gillem and the other soldiers were there for the purpose of forcing the Modoc chief and his followers back onto the Klamath reservation. The chief's name was Kei-in-to-poses but the whites called him "Captain Jack."

Colonel Gillem had once been the military director for Mississippi and Arkansas after the Civil War. He had no particular skill for the job and his military record was mediocre at best. His only qualification was that he shared a close friendship with President Andrew Johnson. Gillem and the president were known to enjoy a cigar and a drink that would last well into the night. Johnson gave him the job and ignored all the concerns about Gillem's record and conduct. General Grant took office as

President of the United States in 1869 and fired Gillem on his first day in office. Gillem was also linked to postwar corruption in the South.

Gillem reverted to his permanent rank of colonel and sent out west. He was passed from one frontier post to another until he landed at Benicia Barracks in northern California where he was given command of the First U.S. Cavalry. He always began drinking rye whiskey as soon as he got up in the morning and continued until he dropped sometime that night. He was known for being mercenary and ill tempered as well as being notoriously shy of combat.

York reported to Gillem at the ranch house that evening. The colonel was drinking from a tin cup when York arrived. The black hair on his head was receding but he still wore a long, full beard. His dark brown eyes were glossy and bloodshot.

"Ya looky here, Lieutenant," Gillem said as he wagged his finger in front of unfocused eyes. "Ya better git my friends up here without no Injuns scalping 'em. They're real important folks to me. Ya understand? They're close friends of Colonel Davis and Mr. Jesse Carr." Gillem spoke with a threatening tone in his voice.

"No problem, sir. We'll get them here easily," York replied.

"Now you and your scouts follow Captain Hurtsell here. He'll see to it that ya get somethin' to eat and a place to bed down for tonight. You boys get on down to Crescent City tomorrow and wait for my special guests." Gillem chuckled a little as he chatted about his "special guests."

Captain Hurtsell rose from his seat and approached the men in the center of the room. The crafty officer was a small, slender man with long string-like black hair. He had a narrow face with slight depressions at either cheek. He didn't smile much but when he did there was a generous display of darkened teeth.

"Bring yer men and foller me," Hurtsell said with a sly smile.

"Yeah, you follow him. Hurtsell has been my right hand goin' all the way back to the war," Gillem said as he smiled at the two officers.

York and Hurtsell left the ranch house and collected the rest of the lieutenant's detachment. As the soldiers led their horses to the corral Hurtsell began to ask questions. "Say, any of you uns like to play poker?" he asked with a sly look on his face. "I put together a little game now and then. We'd take kindly to ya joinin' us when ya can."

Before York could respond Billy answered the question. "Sure I'll play. Have ya got any whiskey a man can buy?"

York looked at Billy with disappointment on his face. Then he turned back to Hurtsell. "No. We will not play cards tonight and there'll be no drinking either. We have to leave at sunup and it's already late."

The York scouts all camped in tents provided by Gillem's troops. They were up early and in the saddle not long after daylight.

The air was cool and crisp as the sun rose behind them. The scenery was beyond description as the men crossed the Siskiyou Range bound for the coast. The peaks of the mountains seemed to brush the clouds above them. The brilliant blue of the sky took on a deeper hue in the brightness of the morning sun.

Soon they were at a point where the vast Pacific Ocean came into view. It was late in the afternoon when they arrived in Crescent City. The money provided by the army allowed Lieutenant York to put his men up at the boarding house on the west edge of town.

The next morning York took Billy and Rattler with him to the docks. The little port was a buzz of activity with fishermen and traders preparing for their day. Small waves lapped at the docks and the air smelled of salt and fish.

York found his party preparing to load two wagons. "My name is Lieutenant Paul York. I've been sent here to assist your travel to Yreka," the young lieutenant said using his most official tone.

"Oh yes, we've been expecting you," the younger man said as he extended his hand. "I'm from the War Department in Washington; my name is Wilburn White. May I please introduce Frederick Von Schlyke of Prussia, I'm escorting him on a scientific expedition." White gestured toward the little man beside him.

A strange, dwarf-like bald man stepped forward to shake the lieutenant's hand. He wore glasses with tiny wire circles holding the lenses of his spectacles. He was only about four and a half feet tall with a thin mustache cutting a straight line above his upper lip. His native language was German but he spoke broken English.

As he shook the young lieutenant's hand he bowed his head slightly in a formal presentation.

"Could your men assist with the loading of our wagons, please?" White asked.

Mr. White and Lieutenant York made small talk while the soldiers loaded Von Schlyke's scientific cargo onto the wagons. Von Schlyke fluttered about the men screeching in German. He insisted that the men take extra care with his cargo. Due to the scientist's interference it took over two hours to load the wagons.

As soon as everyone was ready York put Billy and Rattler out front and the odd procession departed the coast and headed inland. The two dignitaries rode in a buggy directly behind the wagons.

York rode up beside Billy and Rattler laughing as he approached. "Man, that German fellow is a strange one, isn't he?"

"Yeah, he sure is," Billy replied. "Ya should have seen some of his gear. One of them boxes popped open and it was full of knives and little saws. Say, Yorkie, yer a smart Yankee, what kind of whisky is firm-dee-hyde?" Billy asked. "That scientist feller has several little barrels of it. Is it good whiskey?" Billy inquired further.

"I think you mean formaldehyde. I saw it stamped on the barrels. I don't know for sure, but I think undertakers use it. I don't think you want to drink that," York replied.

"You reckon this Von Schlyke is an undertaker? I've heard of 'em picklin' a dead man with that stuff." Billy continued while York and Rattler listened. "Then there was clear glass pickle jars, great big ones. They was packed in straw with big ole' glass lids packed separate. I thought they was for holding whiskey."

"Well, maybe he's collecting specimens like insects, birds, and animals to take back for science," York said as he plodded along beside his two friends.

"If that's what he's doin' he collectin' some pretty big samples. Them jars are big enough to hold a watermelon," Billy joked.

Chapter Thirty

—— NOVEMBER 15, 1872 ——

Yreka, California
Billy and Rattler found themselves living in relative luxury at the boarding house. York stayed down the street at the Yreka Hotel. They were to remain in town awaiting further orders.

Billy and Rattler were told to look after the horses and keep themselves out of trouble. The next morning they fed the horses and checked on all their gear before starting for the hotel to find York.

When they turned the corner Billy bumped into a young native woman carrying two sizable boxes. She screeched and dropped her packages.

"Howdy, ma'am," Billy said as he touched the brim of his hat.

Rattler picked up the boxes while Billy and the young native stared at each other.

"My name is Billy," he said, extending his hand.

There was no response from her at first but then she spoke very softly. "I am called Loma. I work for Mrs. Roseborough."

The young lady was beautiful. She was built like other women of her tribe tending to be short and a little broader in the hips. Her cheekbones were set a bit high on an otherwise perfectly formed face. Her dark skin contrasted beautifully with the brilliant white of her teeth. She was well groomed and wore a dark brown dress that touched the top of her moccasins. The dress was decorated with fine native beadwork stitched around the neck and sleeves. Her jet black hair was bundled under a tule basket hat commonly worn by Modoc women.

Her brown eyes glittered as she flicked her eyelashes and smiled back at Billy. She looked at Rattler with apparent curiosity. "You are an Indian soldier?" she asked.

Rattler started to answer but Billy beat him to it. At this point Billy took off his hat. "Yes, ma'am, he's an Indian soldier; he's a Cherokee. We're scouts for the U.S. Army."

"Cheer-a-Kee. I do not know such a tribe," Loma said.

Billy and Rattler insisted on carrying the boxes while they escorted her to the home of Judge Roseborough.

"It's a mighty fine pleasure to meet you. Loma. Can I come see ya sometime?" Billy asked as politely as he knew how.

The young woman only giggled and disappeared through the little gate and into the house.

"She's a pretty thing, ain't she, Rattler?"

"She pretty, she good spirit, very good spirit," Rattler responded.

"Loma is about the prettiest thing I've ever seen." Billy looked toward the window hoping to catch another glimpse of her.

The next day Billy went to the edge of town where the judge lived. He waited for over two hours hoping to encounter the beautiful native girl he'd met the day before. Finally his prayers were answered; she appeared on the front porch with a broom in her hand. Billy bounded off the pine log he was sitting on and walked straight to the Roseborough's house. He had just reached forward to open the gate when she saw him coming. Her striking brown eyes opened wide when she recognized the young man she'd collided with the day before. She covered her mouth with her hand to hide her smile and her embarrassment.

Billy opened the gate and walked onto the porch and stood facing her only a foot away. He took off his hat before he spoke. "Well, I'll be darned! I was just passin' by when I saw you on the porch. I'm glad I got to see you again, Loma." Billy grinned. "Can we sit a while here on the porch? Me bein' in the army and all, well, I thought ya might teach me a little about this country."

Loma now held both hands over her mouth and giggled uncontrollably. Billy watched as she tried to speak but she seemed to be so embarrassed that words would not come.

At age twenty-five Billy had practically no experience with women, other than a few drunken experiences in San Francisco. Her embarrassment began to unnerve him.

Loma was nineteen years old but she appeared much younger to Billy. She was so pretty. "You can talk if you want to. I won't bother ya none," Billy said as he tried to appear in control of himself.

For a moment both parties were at a loss for words, but the uncomfortable silence was interrupted by Mrs. Roseborough's appearance on the front porch.

"Loma? Is there a problem here?" the older woman asked while staring at Billy.

"Oh, no, ma'am. It's the soldier I told you about yesterday."

"Could we help you with something, young man?" Mrs. Roseborough asked Billy.

"Well, ma'am, I was wonderin' if it would be OK with you and the judge if I came to call on Miss Loma," Billy said as if he were making a speech before Congress.

At that moment it seemed to be the most important thing in Billy's life. Mrs. Roseborough seemed to accept him with mild amusement. She turned back to see a beaming smile on the young girl's face.

"What's your name, young man?" the stately woman asked.

"Long, ma'am. William Nicholas Long, from North Carolina. But everybody just calls me Billy."

"My, you're a long way from home, aren't you?"

"Oh, yes. I came west with the army at the end of the war. Been somewhere out west ever since. Reckon I'll be stayin' in these parts."

"If you want to talk to Loma I suggest you join us for dinner. Let's say next Sunday?"

Billy's demeanor changed as he beamed with excitement.

"Oh, yes, ma'am! I'll be here next Sunday," Billy said as he turned to look at the embarrassed young lady watching the conversation. "I'll see you next Sunday, Miss Loma." He put his hat on, dashed down the steps, and waved back to the two women on the porch.

"Oh, Mr. Long, wouldn't you like to know what time to be here?" Mrs. Roseborough asked with a chuckle.

"Oh yeah, sure. What time?"

"Be here at five p.m. That will give you and Mr. Roseborough a chance to chat before dinner."

"I'll be here, right on time!"

When Billy returned to the Roseborough home on Sunday he found Loma wearing a pretty blue western dress. It had long sleeves and white lace around a high collar. She looked beautiful to Billy as she exposed a little smile.

Judge A. M. Roseborough approached the young soldier and extended his hand. "You must be Mr. Long."

"Yes, sir. Billy Long, sir."

"Come, let's have a seat in the parlor."

The two men sat in the formal parlor and attempted to carry on a conversation. Billy was uncomfortable and distracted as the judge began to question him about his past.

"Have you been in California for some time?" the judge inquired.

"Yes, sir, a few years now. We were at Benicia Barracks for a while, then we got ordered up here. We're scouts, ya know."

"Yes, I understood that," the judge said.

"My good friend John Rattler is the best tracker in the army. Me and him come out here together. He's a Cherokee; well, he's a Snowbird really, but the Snowbirds are a part of the Cherokee tribe."

"If you're from North Carolina how did you end up out here? It's a long way from North Carolina to California," the judge asked with growing curiosity.

Billy told his story of how he had been conscripted as a Junior Reserve in the Confederate army, captured, and sent to prison. He told the judge of his "Galvanized" conversion and his decision to stay in the army.

Mrs. Roseborough called the men to dinner and the party of four sat at a large table with Loma and Billy sitting opposite each other.

The meal was a delightful change for Billy. He was used to eating army food, trail food, and lousy hotel food. This meal was of fresh meat, canned vegetables, and hot bread.

Loma said little and ate even less. She sat and listened as the judge and Mrs. Roseborough continued to question the young soldier about his past.

When the last of their meal was consumed the judge invited Billy back to the parlor for a cigar. The judge sat in an ornate chair with cigar in hand. He drew smoke from his cigar then blew it softly into the air as he continued his evaluation of the young suitor. "You seem to have taken a high interest in Loma."

"Yes, sir, she's a mighty fine girl. I'd like to call on her some," Billy said as he carefully considered his words.

"Maybe you can call on her some but you may want to know a little more about her," the judge said.

"Yes, I'd like that," Billy replied.

"Not many people in these parts know it but Loma came to us as an infant. We've done our best to care for her and raise her as a Christian girl.

"To understand her story you have to go back sixteen years to the time when she was just a toddler. It was shortly after white people began to move into this area; the year was 1856. After a period of conflict settlers and Indians began to live in harmony."

Roseborough paused and studied Billy's face. He could tell that he had Billy's full attention as he continued the story. "A man named Ben Wright organized a militia and they called themselves Oregon Volunteers. Wright called himself captain even though he held no real rank. Wright befriended the Modoc chief and invited him and his tribe to a big feast and a talk.

"The Modoc chief brought his whole tribe to the camp on the south side of Lost River near a place they call Natural Bridge. He asked the Indians to camp on the riverbank while he and his men set up their camp, with the Indians between them and the river.

"A big feast was held that night and all were contented. The Modoc chief told his people that they had found new friends among the whites. The Modocs all slept peacefully with their stomachs full. More than two-thirds of them were women and children.

"Just before daylight Wright's men began to stir. Of about one hundred men in his party, twenty-five or so left the camp. All of the whites had loaded their weapons and moved to predetermined positions in the camp. When the Modoc chief rose from his rest he sought out Ben Wright. As he approach his new friend Wright pulled a revolver and shot the chief dead and called out his orders for the killing to begin.

"Within seconds all of the Indians were up and scrambling for safety. Some of the warriors tried to get their bows strung but it was too late. Wright and his men began to shoot them down. Some of the Modocs tried to escape but the Oregon Volunteers had the way blocked.

"The only way out seemed to be for the surviving Indians to jump into the river. The Modoc chief's wife had a baby with her only about two years old. She ran screaming to the river carrying her baby. But she was shot down before she could make it to the water. One of Wright's men came and grabbed up the baby and prepared to slash the baby's throat. Before the deed could be done a Modoc boy of only thirteen years knocked the man down and took the baby from him.

"The Modoc boy dashed down the bank and into the river as the

Oregon men continued to shoot and kill the Modocs. When the boy went into the river other Modocs were already swimming in the water.

"The boy thought he had reached safety but the ordeal was not over. The twenty-five men of Wright's party who had left before daylight were now positioned on the north bank of the Lost River waiting on the Modocs. They began shooting the Indians dead in the water as they tried to escape the carnage.

"The young Modoc boy saw this. He held onto the little baby and dove into the water. He swam downstream with bullets flying all around him. Finally he made it downstream far enough to get out of the water and make his escape. To this day the incident is known as the Ben Wright Massacre."

Roseborough seemed to finish his tale when he stopped to puff on his cigar.

"That don't sound to good to me. I reckon it ain't no wonder that Indians don't trust white people," Billy said shaking his head.

"There is more that you should know," Roseborough said as he leaned forward and looked Billy straight in the eye. "The young Modoc boy was Captain Jack, the chief's son. He is the man you and the other soldiers have been sent here to capture. He is chief of the Modocs. Captain Jack is a strong leader and an honorable man," Roseborough said with confidence.

"I reckon maybe we won't have no fightin' this time. Maybe it can all be worked out," Billy said as he considered the whole affair.

"There's one more thing, young man. The little girl that Captain Jack saved at Lost River was Loma. Loma is his half-sister; she is a daughter of the Modoc chief. Loma is a Modoc princess." Roseborough finished his remarks, then watched Billy carefully.

Billy stood up and stared at the judge with his eyes wide open. He put his hands over his face for a moment, then slid them away. "Oh my God, I might not have ever known her."

He began to thank God mentally for saving Loma as he turned away from Roseborough. Then his relief turned to anger. He gritted his teeth and blurted out a question that he knew Roseborough couldn't answer. "Where in God's name was the U.S. Army when all this was happening?"

Chapter Thirty-One

—— NOVEMBER 20, 1872 ——

Lava Beds, Northern California
John Rattler carefully steered his horse over the rough rocky surface of the beds. He worked his way to a high point overlooking the valley. Travel here was painfully slow. The experienced army scout was forced to dismount and lead his horse.

Rattler had never seen anything like it. It was a vast landscape of cool molten rock as far as the eye could see. It went on for miles. He painstakingly turned his horse around and began to lead her out of the stone landscape.

The men were sent to scout the area to the south of the lava beds below Tule Lake. Their mission was to coordinate army maps and to look for discrepancies with civilian maps. As Rattler left the lava field he contemplated what he had just seen. Rattler knew that the famous Captain Jack was in there somewhere on the north end of the field. They were scouting with specific orders not to engage the Modocs.

Rattler remounted and rode back to meet Lieutenant York, Billy and the other soldiers. The men pulled their horses to a stop while Rattler reported on what he'd seen.

He began shaking his head. "Is very bad. I never seen like it," Rattler said.

"So I reckon it's as bad as they say?" York commented.

All of them had heard of the harsh conditions in the lava beds but they believed the claims to be exaggerated.

"Is bad spirit there, very bad," Rattler said with an expression that attracted the other men's attention. "I can no track in there. Stone hard everywhere." Rattler moved his hand slowly through the air trying to indicate that he was talking about a vast land. He turned and pointed toward the lava, then turned back to face the men. "In there, no see. Maybe as far as two horses, maybe none."

York and Rattler dismounted and spent the day exploring the south end of the lava bed fields. They reached one certain conclusion. There could be no direct approach to Captain Jack's stronghold from the south.

When the men returned to Yreka, Billy called on the Roseboroughs and Loma the very next day. After a brief visit he returned to the boarding house to announce that all three of them had been invited to the Roseboroughs' for dinner the next evening.

Rattler was amused at how excited Billy was about the upcoming event. Billy went to the general store and bought cologne and a new bandanna to go around his neck. Billy and Rattler put on clean uniforms and headed for the hotel to meet York.

"I tell ya, she's the prettiest thing I ever saw. Ain't she Rattler?" Billy said.

Rattler smiled and nodded his head. Both he and York chuckled with amusement as Billy raved about his new love interest.

The three men began a brisk walk and headed for the Roseboroughs' house. They had just left the hotel when York raised his nose to the air and wrinkled his face.

"What's that damn smell?" he said in apparent confusion.

The normally laconic Rattler burst out with laughter as York turned in every direction attempting to sniff out the unpleasant odor.

"Cattle roll in mud, keep bugs off. White men roll in pee," he said as he pointed at Billy and laughed.

Billy took immediate offense and snapped back at Rattler. "It ain't pee; it's cologne from France. It's for men," Billy said defending himself.

York looked confused at first, then leaned over closer to Billy and took in a big whiff of air. "Damn, it's you!" York said as he quickly moved away from Billy.

York looked at Rattler and the two men began laughing hysterically.

"What's so damn funny? You two don't have no girls, do ya?"

York looked at Billy, and then took another sniff from a safer distance; his eyes rolled then focused on Rattler. "Well I'll be damned, it is pee," York said with great enthusiasm.

Billy raised his fist and threatened his two friends.

"You two better not say nothin' to embarrass me in front of Loma," Billy said in a voice that indicated he was really getting upset.

York and Rattler promised to behave and the trio continued on to the Roseborough home.

When they arrived Mrs. Roseborough greeted them at the door. Rattler was always uncomfortable in such settings but York was at ease.

Mrs. Roseborough led them to the parlor where the judge sat waiting. The men were discussing the current Indian trouble when Loma entered the room. She wore the same blue dress she'd worn before, but she looked even more beautiful.

Rattler watched his best friend as Billy beamed with pride. Loma looked at Billy and smiled. After the introductions were completed Mrs. Roseborough called them all to the table.

As they walked down the hallway York turned to Billy and whispered carefully. "My, my Billy. She's even prettier than you said. She's beautiful."

Billy's eyes brightened as he smiled at York. "I told ya so."

The judge sat at the head of the table and talked of his travels and experiences on the bench. At one point he wrinkled his nose and asked Mrs. Roseborough what the strange smell was but she had no answer. Rattler stared at his plate as the pair of soldiers fought to contain their laughter.

Rattler watched Billy and Loma as the night went on. The two appeared to engage the others but Rattler could see that they were only truly interested in each other. They constantly glanced back and forth exchanging smiles and looks.

After the evening meal was completed the judge called York and Rattler to the parlor. Billy went to the front porch with Loma.

Roseborough and the young officer took to each other immediately. The judge quizzed him on everything the army was doing and York attempted to learn everything he could about the town. Rattler just sat in silence looking and feeling uncomfortable.

"What do you think the army really wants out of this whole affair with the Modocs?" the judge asked the lieutenant.

"We just want the Modocs to go back to their reservation, I guess," York said as he quoted the army's public position. He thought for a minute then shook his head. "Really, sir, I don't know. I just follow orders and scout whatever they tell me to scout."

Rattler watched and listened carefully. He didn't know what the army was up to but he was confident that it was not anything good.

"There is a rich and powerful man named Jesse Carr who is after the Modocs' land. He has many politicians and army officers on his payroll. He is corrupt and dishonest. He has this plan called Stock Ranchero. Basically he plans to control all the stock land in northern California. He wants land but the army is after something else?" Roseborough said in a suspicious manner.

"But what could the Modocs have that the army would want?" York asked.

"I don't know but they're after something," Roseborough said. "Have you met Mr. White from the War Department in Washington?"

"Yes, we escorted him and some German fellow up from the coast," York replied.

Roseborough's eyes lit up when Von Schlyke was mentioned. "It's that Mr. Von Schlyke, that German gentleman, who caught my attention.

They claim he is a scientist. He is quite the odd fellow," Roseborough said. "Mr. White, Colonel Gillem, and Von Schlyke were all here for dinner a while back. We offered them some wine and they drank everything in the house. They all had too much to drink and when we were having our cigars Von Schlyke began screaming at Colonel Gillem and White. He was talking about how he was going to make great scientific discoveries; he went on and on about how important it was that his cargo not be damaged. But he didn't say what he had in mind." The judge continued as if it were all a mystery.

"The thing that bothered Mrs. Roseborough the most was how he kept looking at Loma. His eyes would follow her around the room; then he would mumble something in German," Roseborough said; his tone revealed his trepidation.

Rattler listened in silence but when the judge was finished talking he spoke for the first time. "Men full of bad spirits."

Both men looked at Rattler and considered what he said. Then York spoke up. "We carried a lot of freight for the man, but neither he nor Mr. White told us what they were collecting."

"I was just hoping you might shed some light on the matter," the judge said.

"They didn't tell us anything but Rattler and Billy did take notice of one thing. Von Schlyke's cargo included some big clear-glass pickle jars. But they made no secret of it.

"There was one other thing, now that I think about it. We loaded several small barrels of formaldehyde onto their wagons."

Chapter Thirty-Two

—— NOVEMBER 29, 1872 ——

Portland, Oregon
Lieutenant Paul York rode into town with only John Rattler for company. York left Billy Long on duty in Yreka just so he could be with his sweetheart. Both York and Rattler knew that Billy was in love, and both men were happy for him. York knew how Billy had suffered in prison and Rattler had suffered right along with him.

"No one deserves happiness any more than Billy," York told his Cherokee friend.

York was anxious about his trip to Portland. The commanding general of the Department of the Columbia, General E. R. S. Canby, had summoned him. Canby was a man known to "go by the book" when implementing the wishes of Washington. He always tried to follow the rules and carry out army policy in accordance with War Department directives.

When York arrived at army headquarters in Portland he instructed Rattler to wait while he reported to General Canby.

York walked into the building where he was greeted by a young enlisted man. He was given a seat and told to wait. It was over an hour before he was called into General Canby's office.

York walked into the room, saluted, then stood at attention.

"At ease, Lieutenant," General Canby said with a wave of his hand. "Have a seat while we discuss the situation with the Modocs."

Canby walked around to the front of his desk taking a cigar from a wooden box as he passed. He sat down in the chair next to York and lit the cigar.

"Lieutenant, do you know why I called you up from Benicia Barracks?"

"I think so, sir; it was because you needed scouts…good trackers?" York responded with some doubt.

"Yes, yes, we did need the service of trackers but there was more to it," Canby said calmly. "I needed someone to report directly to me. Someone who could be, shall we say, a little more independent. Someone who was not beholden to Colonel Davis and Colonel Gillem." Canby paused while he gathered his thoughts. "There is something going on with the War Department and two men they sent out here. One of them is a German fellow who is some kind of scientist."

York listened intently as the general continued to brief him on the situation.

"They've ordered me to bring in Colonel Davis and Colonel Gillem. Not that I object, but it does make me wonder. It's highly unusual to be assigned high-ranking officers without any consultation."

"Did you not approve of their assignment here?" York asked.

"No, I'm afraid not. I was not consulted," Canby replied.

"I see that, but what does that have to do with me?"

"I want you to report directly to me by way of telegraph or courier. I want someone watching my back. I want to see if you can figure out what Mr. White and the Baron Von Schlyke are up to. That little fellow didn't come all the way from Germany to collect butterflies," the general said with a cough. "I have been informed that Colonel Davis and Colonel Gillem are on Jesse Carr's payroll. They are taking bribes. You are to tell no one of this assignment. You will operate in secret as a special intelligence officer under my protection."

CHAPTER THIRTY-TWO

General Canby kept York for over two hours while they discussed the sad history of America's Indian wars.

"First, we had that awful slaughter of Modocs at Bloody Point some years back. Then when we put the Modocs on the Klamath Reservation, that didn't work. The Klamaths treated them worse than whites did. Since then both sides have had some of their folks doing the wrong thing. It's got to stop somewhere," the general said.

Canby turned and looked directly at York, took the cigar out of his mouth and spoke firmly. "You know, Lieutenant York, my wife is a woman with a soft heart and a good mind. She cares about people who've had a hard time in life. She's made me think about what I've done and what we've done as a people. Now I lie awake at night and think of what I did as a young man. Let's just say I have some painful regrets. Maybe I'm getting a little softer as I get older." The general puffed on his cigar again.

"The War Department doesn't seem to have much consideration for any natives," York said.

"You have a Cherokee scout with you, don't you, Lieutenant?" Canby asked.

"Yes, sir, he was a Confederate soldier who became a Galvanized Yankee at the end of the war."

"When I was a young second lieutenant, just out of West Point, my first duty was to join in the removal of the Cherokees. It was terrible. They were given little food and no shelter while on the trail to Oklahoma. All of them were driven from their homes except for small bands that hid out in the mountains of western North Carolina." Canby rose from his chair and walked over to the window.

York bowed his head but said nothing as the general stared out the window and continued talking.

"I watched many of them die on the trail. Some died of disease, others died of exposure, but some seemed to die of sadness. It was such a waste. I'm going to do everything in my power to prevent any more unnecessary loss of life. We've got to give the Indians a fair chance."

Canby dismissed York and sent him on his way. York and Rattler were given quarters at the army barracks in Portland. They put up their horses and enjoyed a good meal of beef stew and cornbread at the army barracks. They were just finishing their meal when an enlisted man came into the building and called York back to the commanding general's office.

"You are to report immediately," the soldier told him.

York returned to Canby's office to find the general in a highly agitated state.

"Lieutenant York, I just got a telegram from northern California. Major Jackson was sent to see if he could get Captain Jack and his Modoc followers to return to the reservation. Some of the soldiers got spooked and started shooting," Canby said with disgust. "Worse than that, Major Jackson encouraged some civilians to go to the other Modoc camp at Hooker Jim's village. I suppose you know those damn civilians started shooting too. Now we've got a full-fledged Indian war going on." Canby demonstrated his anger by slamming his hand on the desk.

While they were talking a courier came in with another telegram from northern California. It was the casualty report from Major Jackson. One soldier was killed in the fight but seven others were wounded, one of whom died later. The report boasted that they had killed several Modocs. Two civilians were killed and several more wounded at Hooker Jim's camp.

Later reports indicated that the Lost River Battle had resulted in several Modocs being killed, mostly women and children. Only one Modoc warrior was killed and one wounded.

But that was not the worst news as Lieutenant York saw it. "Sir, Captain Jack will certainly retreat to the lava beds. General Canby, sir, I've never seen any ground worse than that. If Captain Jack is half the warrior they say he is, many a good man will have to die if we go in there after him."

Chapter Thirty-Three

—— APRIL 10, 1873 ——

Lava Beds, Northern California
John Rattler and Billy Long waited by a smoldering fire while York met with General Canby. Nearly six months had passed since the Modoc War started. Captain Jack had held off an army with only fifty-five warriors, all the while burdened with a band of women and children. The army had suffered sixty-eight killed and seventy-five wounded on their side. The Modocs had lost several warriors and a number of women and children.

How in God's name did it come to this? Billy wondered.

Things had gotten so bad that General Canby had come to the lava beds to personally lead a Peace Commission. He hoped to talk the Modocs into a workable settlement. He felt a moral obligation to attempt a peaceful settlement even at his own risk.

York and his scout detachment were given secondary roles by Colonel Gillem but they were still in a position to see much of what transpired.

———

Billy left the campfire to find his way to the latrine. On the return he circled by the officers tents where merchants and other vendors dallied with soldiers and journalists alike. Civilians and camp followers of every description invaded the perimeter. Whiskey, money, and words flowed freely through the night air.

Rumors abounded that the Modocs planned to kill the peace commissioners, including General Canby. Most of these reports were dismissed by Colonel Gillem, as irrational or panic-driven. Billy Long and Lieutenant York were not so confident.

When Billy passed behind Gillem's tent he was stopped by a guard but allowed to pass once his identity was determined. Billy glanced between the tents where he caught sight of Colonel Gillem and his personal assistant, Captain Hurtsell, standing by the fire. Gillem was in a heated conversation with Mr. White from the War Department and the scientist Von Schlyke. Billy crept closer and stood quietly between the two tents. Soon he could hear their conversation. Another officer unfamiliar to Billy was also there. It was Colonel Jefferson Columbus Davis.

"Leave this to me, gentleman; everything is going according to your wishes," Colonel Davis assured the two civilians.

"I must have zamples undamaged," Von Schlyke shrieked.

"I told you I'd take care of everything," Davis assured him. "We'll take care of your needs and Mr. Carr's all at the same time."

"It must be a complete zample, vith zee royal blood. Zee scientific vorld depends on it," he continued.

Davis and Gillem left the site while Von Schlyke continued to utter his concerns to Mr. White, as the War Department representative.

"Vhat azzurance do vee have? Vhat do vee do if Colonel Gillem is relieved or killed?" the little scientist asked White.

"You don't have to worry about that. Colonel Gillem will have to be relieved after the killing, but Colonel Davis will replace him. He will cooperate fully. As for Gillem being killed?" White laughed as he said it. "Colonel Gillem is known for avoiding combat. He will not go anywhere near a Modoc. He'd run from a squaw with a spoon."

Billy slipped back out between the tents and returned to Rattler at their campfire. Lieutenant York arrived shortly thereafter.

"Hey, Yorkie, there're a lot of strange things going on around here," Billy told him as if he were totally confused.

"I know. I've seen some pretty strange things myself. One of the Modoc warriors is in camp. It's Bogus Charley; he's been talking to that Colonel Davis and Captain Hurtsell a lot. I wonder what's he doing here the night before the big peace council," York said. "I thought they were at war with us?"

"I don't know but I walked by Gillem's tent. He had that scary Captain Hurtsell along with White and Von Schlyke in some kind of fuss," Billy said. "The little German was wailing about his samples and somethin' else." Billy continued to recount the whole thing as clearly as possible, hoping his friend could shed some light on the matter.

"Another thing. That War Department feller said Gillem would be replaced. How come he said that?" Billy asked York.

"Bad spirits always in bad heart," Rattler warned them.

"What did General Canby say?" Billy asked.

"He called in Colonel Gillem and told him that our scout detachment is to move in behind the peace tent without being seen. We're to get as close as possible in case something goes wrong," York told them quietly. "If any trouble starts we're to move in quickly. We'll come up behind the peace tent and hide in the sagebrush. Colonel Gillem will then move up in force if necessary."

The three old friends sat around the fire and checked and cleaned their weapons while they talked.

"Hey fellers, I've got somethin' to tell ya. Me and Loma are gonna get married. We're gonna have a sure enough church weddin' with a preacher and all. I want you two to be there with me," Billy said with a tear in his eye.

Rattler smiled and slapped his old friend on the back. York threw his hands in the air and shouted hallelujah.

"Time has come, my brother. Beautiful woman no wait forever," Rattler said with a laugh.

"Good for you, Billy. You two will have a wonderful life," York said as he sat on the other side of Billy and shook his hand.

"Her father is dead, so I was kinda hopin' you'd walk her down the aisle for me. You bein' an officer and all," Billy said as his lip quivered.

"Shouldn't Judge Roseborough or John do that? Rattler has been your best friend since you two were in the Confederate army," York said not wanting to hurt Rattler's feelings.

"Naw, he can't. He's gonna be the best man. I talked to the judge about it and he wants you to do it." Billy turned and looked Rattler in the eye. Both men began to tear up.

"One good thing for you, Lieutenant, me and Rattler'll be leavin' when our enlistments are up," Billy said with some sadness.

"If it's the best thing for you, then I'm happy for you both. Besides, I won't have to bail Billy out of jail anymore." York chuckled, and Billy and Rattler laughed with him.

"Let's bed down and take care of business tomorrow. Then we'll celebrate the good news when we get back to Yreka," York said with genuine happiness in his voice.

All three scouts slept intermittently as they anticipated their duty for the coming day. When they arose the next morning they found others stirring about. Camp sutler Pat McManus was selling everything he could. Soldiers and reporters chatted among the tents. There was an eerie circus-like atmosphere in the camp.

At eleven a.m. General Canby left Gillem's camp for the peace council tent along with Mr. Meacham, Mr. Dyar, Reverend Thomas, two interpreters, and the two Modoc warriors who had stayed at Gillem's camp the night before—Boston Charley and Bogus Charley. York and the other scouts watched them leave. The peace council site was only a few hundred yards away from Gillem's camp.

As they exited the camp, Modoc warrior Bogus Charley looked back at Captain Hurtsell. There was a nod from the soldier, and an acknowledgment from Bogus Charley. Billy saw this and whispered to York. "Did you see that?"

"Yeah. We'd better move into position. Something isn't right here," York said quietly.

Billy and Rattler checked their weapons as they followed York toward their assigned post. Tension gripped them all as they prepared for the worst. Billy and Rattler had been soldiers in two armies for nearly a decade but neither of them had ever fired on another human being. Both men were filled with apprehension as they prepared for trouble.

"Lieutenant York, hold up thar."

Billy turned to see who was calling them. Captain Hurtsell scurried up to them accompanied by about a dozen soldiers from the First Cavalry. The other men all carried carbines and Hurtsell had his revolver strapped on his hip.

"Colonel Gillem sent me to fetch you. There's been a change in yer orders. You are to plant yerself right here and stay," Hurtsell told them with a sly smile.

"No, I'm afraid I can't do that. I got my orders from General Canby," York told him firmly.

"General Canby ain't here. Colonel Gillem is in command now," Hurtsell insisted. "You'll have to bring yer men and come with me." Hurtsell sounded impatient.

"I can't disobey orders from General Canby. I'm sure Colonel Gillem will understand," York said as he turned his back on Hurtsell and ordered Rattler and Billy to follow him.

"Lieutenant, stop right thar! I've got orders from Colonel Gillem to bring ya back," Hurtsell shouted.

"I have to go. General Canby may be in danger!" York shouted back at him.

Hurtsell turned his head and called to one of the cavalrymen. "Corporal, take these here men under guard and disarm them!"

York, Billy, and Rattler stood shocked, unsure of what was happening. In an instant, other soldiers in blue surrounded the scouts. The cavalrymen stood pointing their carbines at them while still others confiscated their weapons.

"You men foller me. If ya cause any trouble you'll be shot," Hurtsell warned them.

The three scouts were escorted under guard back to the officers' tent area. They stood surrounded while Hurtsell whispered something to Gillem. Colonel Gillem glanced over at York and smiled.

Colonel Gillem sat in a field chair and chatted with reporters. From York's point of view he seemed confident and unconcerned.

York, Billy, and Rattler were ordered to sit on the ground while their guards paced around them with declining interest.

"I've got a real bad feelin' about this," Billy said to York as quietly as he could.

"I've got the same feeling. I'm concerned about General Canby," York whispered back to Billy.

"No help general here," Rattler said as if he wanted to try to escape.

"Men, they'd shoot us if we tried to run. I think Colonel Gillem might like that. We can't do anything," York warned.

"They'll have hell to pay when General Canby gets back," Billy said.

York turned to Billy with a look on his face that Billy had never seen before.

"What if General Canby doesn't come back?" York asked Billy.

Within seconds of when York made the comment, a messenger ran up to Colonel Gillem with a signal dispatch from Lieutenant Moore on the east side of the lava beds. The messenger shouted out the message as he handed it to Gillem: Urgent, Modocs attacking, move to protect General Canby immediately! The scouts sat surrounded by their guards but several other officers came forward shouting orders frantically.

"Let's move, men! Secure your weapons!" another officer shouted while running from his tent.

"No, stop right there!" Colonel Gillem shouted at the scrambling soldiers.

"But, sir, General Canby could be in danger," the officer pleaded with Gillem.

"Sir, the dispatch said the Modoc are attacking."

"I have my orders from General Canby. He wants no interference," Gillem shouted at the man.

The officers and their men stood frustrated and confused. Gillem sat in his chair and lit a cigar.

York buried his face in his hands. "Oh God, please forgive me. I'm so sorry," he said as the reality of what was happening sunk in.

Another twelve minutes went by while Gillem sat and slowly recopied the dispatch by hand. Then gunshots were heard coming from the peace tent area but Gillem still refused to allow his men to move.

Another eleven minutes went by before one of the interpreters, Frank Riddle, came running into the camp. He was out of breath, sweating and gasping for air. "They shot General Canby!" he screamed as he ran to Colonel Gillem's tent.

"Hold on there, man, are you sure?" Gillem said calmly while his officers urged him to act.

"Yes, I'm sure, damn it! Bogus Charley cut his throat to make sure he was dead. I saw it as I ran for my life. Dyar and Reverend Thomas are also shot," he screamed.

Gillem seemed to be taking his time as he scratched his chin. By now twenty minutes had gone by.

"What do you think, Captain?" he asked his most agitated officer.

"For God's sake, Colonel, won't you move now?" the man shouted as he tried to control himself.

"No, I will stay here in case I'm needed to coordinate troop movements. You take your men. Go over there and check out Mr. Riddle's report," Gillem said as he calmly strolled back into his tent.

Within minutes confirmation was communicated back to the camp. General Canby was dead.

Chapter Thirty-Four

—— MAY 1, 1873 ——

Fort Klamath, Oregon
Billy Long and Lieutenant York practiced what they intended to say to the new CO for the Department of the Columbia. The officer in this position was in command of all troops in Washington, Oregon, northern California, and Alaska. The War Department announced General Canby's replacement almost immediately. It would be Colonel Jefferson Columbus Davis of Indiana. Even though he shared a name with the former Confederate president, Jefferson Davis of Mississippi, there was no blood relation between the two. He was already in the area and he took command immediately.

Billy and York, along with a most agreeable John Rattler, decided that it would be best not to take their native friend with them to meet the new commander. They knew of suspicious activities and felt bound to report them. Because of their special role with General Canby, York determined that they should only report to the new commander. York wanted Billy there as a witness.

York felt anxious as he considered what he was about to do. Making accusations against a superior officer was serious business and York knew it. The thing that bothered him the most was that he was reporting to an officer he had never met.

"You know the whole horse is on the line here, don't ya?" Billy said.

"Yes, I know that," York responded.

"Happy stay here," Rattler said as he watched them prepare to leave.

There was a knocking at the door that seemed loud and urgent. Tensions were already high inside the barracks that Billy and Rattler shared. Billy opened the door to find Judge Roseborough standing on the top step. He looked tired and ruffled.

There were brief exchanges between them and Billy inquired about Loma. Almost immediately Billy asked the judge why he'd come all the way from Yreka to Fort Klamath?

"I had to come warn you about your new commanding officer. There are things you must know before you talk to him."

Roseborough took a wheezing breath, then continued. "You may remember that as a judge I have a few important contacts here and there. When Davis was selected by the War Department to replace General Canby, I telegraphed my friends in Washington for information on Jefferson Columbus Davis of Indiana. A letter arrived by special courier yesterday."

Roseborough paused to catch his breath before addressing York directly. "I hope to God you haven't said anything to him," the judge said.

"No, but I'm supposed to go over there in a few minutes," York responded.

"Thank God I got here in time," Roseborough said. "You should not say a word to Colonel Davis until you read this. It's the response to my inquiry about him."

"Please don't tell me he's not going to be any better than Colonel Gillem," York said. "Look at the mess we're in! Captain Jack and his men have killed General Canby and the whole U.S. Army can't seem to catch them. No, hell, they've whipped us at every turn."

CHAPTER THIRTY-FOUR

"We have Davis relieving Gillem, more men and more guns. Damn, how much blood do they have to see?" Billy asked Roseborough.

"It's made news all over the country, even in Europe. A small band of Modocs holds off the whole U.S. Army," Roseborough said.

Then the judge handed Lieutenant York the report on Colonel Davis. "I think you'd better read this."

TO THE HONORABLE A.M. ROSEBOROUGH, Confidential
Yreka, California
As to your kind inquiry regarding the personal attributes of one Colonel Jefferson Columbus Davis of the state of Indiana, I respond herewith.

As misfortune sometimes guides us, it seems so in regards to this matter. I utter substantial regret as I say to you that Colonel Davis is a scoundrel of the lowest human kind. He murdered his commanding officer in cold blood in front of many witnesses in 1862. He waited in ambush outside the hotel parlor and shot Major General William Nelson as he walked through the door. He was arrested for the murder, but by means of corrupt political maneuvering the scoundrel was never brought to trial. With the aid of corrupt politicians he was released from arrest after a couple of weeks. Because of a Confederate army under General Bragg pressing the state of Kentucky, a courts marshal was never convened.

In the midst of a desperate war, Davis was returned to duty. He was with General Sherman as they passed over Georgia at the end of the Civil War. Sherman put Jefferson Davis in command of the Union army rear guard. Several thousand freed slaves followed the army. At a place on Ebenezer Creek in Georgia, Sherman's army passed over pontoon bridges.

After the army had passed, freedmen by the hundreds began pouring on to the bridge. Davis cut the ropes on the pontoons. No one knows for sure but there may have been as many as four hundred freed slaves who perished in the water. Most of them were women and children. Davis blamed the deaths on panic and never faced charges. General Sherman didn't seem to care. This incident may qualify Colonel Davis as the worst mass murderer in all American history. Now as General of the Army in Washington, Sherman has put him in command of the Modoc expedition.

I suggest that any interaction with Colonel Davis be approached with extreme caution. Many army officers have known of his murderous tendencies but may have been afraid to criticize Davis. There has been a reasonable fear that they might fall victim to one of his murderous plots. He is an experienced assassin. He is known to be on the payroll of land baron Jesse Carr.

As to caution, I remind you that my letter to you must remain confidential, as this is a dangerous world.
Your most obedient servant,
Sincerely,

York read the letter and noticed that Judge Roseborough had rendered the author's signature unreadable.

"Can you trust the man who wrote this?" York asked.

"Oh yes, he is of impeccable character. I know him to be most reliable," the judge assured him.

"How in God's name could General Sherman have given this command to such a man?" York asked Roseborough.

"General Sherman is a man who wages war without much concern for human life or decency. It seems to me that he favors exterminating all natives," the judge responded.

York went on to his meeting with Colonel Davis but without Billy. He was unsure of what to say or how to conduct himself.

York entered Davis's office while he was preparing to leave for the lava beds to begin his pursuit of Captain Jack and the Modocs. Captain Hurtsell was standing beside the colonel's desk.

"Ya wantin' to see me, Lieutenant?" Colonel Davis asked York when he arrived.

Davis continued shuffling papers and talking to other officers as they came and went. Captain Hurtsell just stared at York and smiled.

"Ah, yes sir. I just wanted to offer my services as a tracker. I thought maybe you could use me." York's voice cracked.

"I don't need no damned tracker, I can find 'em savages on my own. Ya can smell 'em, ya know," Davis said with a glint in his eyes. "We're gonna hunt 'em savages down and kill 'em all."

Davis paused briefly, then looked at Captain Hurtsell. "Except Captain Jack. I want his ass alive. I'm gonna hang his ass. Besides, we don't want him damaged none, do we, Captain Hurtsell?" Davis laughed.

"Now, as fer you, Lieutenant. You are confined to post until further notice. If you need anything you are to report to Captain Hurtsell here," Davis said as he nodded toward Hurtsell. "Now get your ass outta here. I got some Injuns to kill."

York left Davis's office disappointed and confused.

Colonel Jefferson Columbus Davis had arrived at Gillem's camp near the lava beds on May 2, 1873. He had assembled over one thousand men. There were five companies from the U.S. First Cavalry, two companies from the Twelfth Infantry, five companies from the Twenty-first Infantry, and six batteries from the Fourth Artillery. In addition to regular army troops, six companies of Oregon and California militia volunteers supported Davis. He also had over one hundred Indian scouts. Many of the Indian scouts were traditional enemies of the Modocs. Due to losses in battle and desertions Captain Jack and the Modocs were down to fewer than thirty warriors and a cadre of women and children. They were running out of food, water, and time.

Captain Jack and his small band of Modoc warriors landed another blow on the army with a successful attack on a wagon train on May 7. On May 9 Captain Jack delivered still another blow to the army with an attack at Sorass Lake. There were casualties on both side but the battle ended with the Modocs retreating. Modoc warrior Ellen's Man was killed.

While the U.S. Army stumbled around with hundreds of soldiers crossing back and forth in the lava beds, the Modocs began to split. Bogus Charley, the same Modoc who had been in Gillem's Camp the night before General Canby was killed, led the Hot Creek band of Modocs in a split from Captain Jack. Captain Jack led Schonchin John, Black Jim, and the other loyal Modocs on to a new location.

On May 22 U.S. Army detachments caught up with part of the Modoc group near Sheep Mountain. The army attacked and pursued the Modocs; they killed two warriors and three women.

Bogus Charley led a group of sixty-three Modocs, mostly women and children, to Davis's headquarters at Fairchild Ranch and surrendered them to the army. Bogus Charley met with Davis to help plan the capture of Captain Jack. Bogus Charley, the man who killed General Canby, was given a job as an army scout by Colonel Davis. The Modoc War was nearing a conclusion.

Chapter Thirty-Five

—— JUNE 1, 1873 ——

Fort Klamath, Oregon
Billy Long had been AWOL for over a week but Lieutenant York continued to report him "present." He knew Billy was with Loma and he was glad for it. His current disgust with the army only worsened as he continued to get verbal reports from the field. Billy had returned the night before and was back in the barracks with Rattler when York found them.

"Hey, Yorkie, what're we gonna do? Davis has it in for us and that snake Captain Hurtsell looks at us like he's gonna eat us," Billy said with fear in his voice.

"I don't know, Billy, this is all so crazy. I can't figure out what they're up to, but I know it's something big."

John Rattler listened but said little. He had recognized something that Billy had not. Captain Charles Hurtsell was the same Lieutenant Hurtsell who was with Colonel George W. Kirk when Camp Vance was raided in Morganton, North Carolina. Rattler had gotten a good look at his face. He saw him the day the drummer boy was shot in the back.

"We no leave here alive," Rattler said calmly.

"What? Why do ya say that?" Billy asked.

"Unless we go now, Davis kill us," Rattler said as if he knew something.

"Don't say that, John, I'm gonna marry Loma; I love her more than my own life. I ain't gonna let nothin' stop me."

"Then go, my brother. Take her. Leave now. I go with you," Rattler said with conviction.

"You can't do that; the army will track you down for desertion. If they claim a war is on they can have you shot," York warned them.

Billy and Rattler stayed in the barracks while York went to see what reports were coming from the lava beds. The following morning York burst into the barracks where Rattler and Billy were still asleep.

"Wake up, wake up. It's over, Captain Jack surrendered!" York shouted.

"Thank God!" Billy mumbled in response.

"Now maybe we can get back to normal," Billy added.

Rattler raised himself and looked at his two best friends.

"All white men blind. You no see we all die," Rattler said with resignation in his voice.

Rattler looked at Billy and repeated what he had said the day before. "Go, take Loma and run." Then he lay down and rolled over to face the wall.

"Yorkie, can you make him quit saying that? He's spookin' me real bad," Billy said.

York didn't respond, he simply turned and stared out the window.

"What in the hell are they up to?" York said quietly as if talking to no one in particular.

Colonel Davis proceeded with plans to hang Captain Jack and the other Modocs involved in the killing of General Canby immediately. By June fifth Davis had a scaffold built complete with hanging ropes. But before Davis could get them hanged a telegram came from General Sherman. He ordered Davis to put together a military commission and to fake a fair trial for the accused in order to make it appear to be a legal process. The outcome of the military commission's trial was never in doubt.

Despite Davis's lust for blood he mysteriously exempted some Modocs from prosecution. Bogus Charley, the same man who pushed

Captain Jack into going along with his plan to kill Canby, the same man who urged the killing of Canby, the same man who had sliced the general's throat after he was shot, and the same man who had helped bring in Captain Jack was exempted from prosecution by Colonel Davis.

Davis appointed a commission that could not have possibly been more biased. It consisted of Colonel Elliot, First Cavalry; Captain Mendenhall and Hasbrouk, Fourth Artillery; Captain Pollock, Twenty-first Infantry; Lieutenant Kingsbury, Twelfth Infantry; and Major Curtis, judge advocate, Department of California. All the panel members except Curtis had been fighting the Modocs and losing men in battle. Once the military commission was in place it was only a matter of pretense.

The commission began the trial on July 1, 1873. The trial ended on July 9; Captain Jack, Schonchin John, Black Jim, Boston Charley, Barncho, and Slolucx were all found guilty. The sentence was read in open court by Major H. P. Curtis, judge advocate.

"The court orders that all of you shall be hanged by the neck until they be dead."

Chapter Thirty-Six

—— OCTOBER 1, 1873 ——

Fort Klamath, Oregon
Things had loosened up around the fort for York, Billy, and Rattler. Billy felt a bit better about things. Most of all he enjoyed the freedom he was allowed for the purpose of visiting Loma. Billy and Rattler's enlistments were up at the end of November. The couple planned to marry as soon as Billy was out of the army. The happy occasion was to be at the Roseborough home the week before Christmas.

Loma had been separated from her tribe since she was an infant but she was still greatly saddened by the prospect of the Modocs hanging. She experienced nightmares and worried about spirits. She tried to put it out of her mind but found it impossible.

Billy had just returned from a visit with Loma when it was announced that the hanging would take place on the morning of October 3, 1873. The entire army force at Fort Klamath was ordered to assemble in the main yard to witness the hanging. All of the surviving Modocs, including Captain Jack's three-year-old daughter Rosie, were forced to watch the hanging of their leaders and relatives.

Billy rose that morning and dressed as usual. Rattler dressed beside him but there was no conversation between the two. They met York in the yard.

York's scouts were standing at the far left of the main formation. Colonel Davis and Captain Hurtsell stood with a cluster of officers to their right, just in front of the gallows. Modoc women sat on the ground in a cluster just behind the officers.

Billy watched as the prisoners were marched from their cells to the gallows. A slow drumbeat could be heard as a single soldier pounded his instrument to a mournful beat. At first there was only silence, then a low death chant could be heard rising from the Modoc women. One by one the Modoc prisoners were marched to the gallows, none of them resisting. The last to climb the ladder was Captain Jack. At the last minute Barncho and Slolucx were led away, their sentence having been changed to life in prison by President Grant.

As the chief turned to face the soldiers all the spectators got a good look at the famous leader. Even in confinement he was a powerful image standing above the crowd. He stood proud to the end with his shoulders held high and his dark eyes peering into the distance. Lieutenant Kingsbury read the army's order.

Billy looked to his left and saw tears on the face of John Rattler. Both men bowed their heads as the gruesome process continued.

When all were in place Colonel Davis gestured to the officer on the gallows and another enlisted man came forward. For reasons unknown at the time, Davis ordered the soldier to cut the hair off the great leader's head. Davis smiled gleefully as he watched this final humiliation take place. Captain Jack stood silent and motionless as his hair was cut. He only stared into the distance.

Colonel Davis turned to Captain Hurtsell and smiled. "Where's the chief's daughter? Drag that little savage bitch to the front. I want to see the look on her face when she sees her daddy die."

A chaplain prayed as hoods were placed over the heads of the condemned. As this process was undertaken the Modoc women began to chant louder while others began to moan and wail. Once all the condemned were hooded Lieutenant Kingsbury glanced toward Colonel

Davis as if seeking his approval. Davis waved his hand impatiently and laughed as he mumbled, "Get on with it."

One by one the nooses were tied around the necks of the condemned. Another officer came along behind and checked each noose carefully. When satisfied that all were secure Lieutenant Kingsbury looked toward Colonel Davis and he responded with the signal. Another officer held his handkerchief in front of his body. Upon the signal from Davis he dropped the handkerchief.

At 10:20 a.m. the rope holding the drop was cut. The four Modocs dropped through and fell with a thud. There was a gasp from the spectators and a wail of anguish went up from the Modocs. Many of the soldiers turned away or looked at each other in disgust. Rosie Jack stood sobbing quietly as she watched her father sway in the wind.

Colonel Davis giggled with delight as he watched. Captain Jack and Black Jim succumbed quickly but Schonchin John and Boston Charley jerked and quivered in apparent convulsions. Colonel Davis delighted in their suffering. Davis leaned over to whisper to Hurtsell. "Damn, I wanted to see Jack squirm."

The bodies swung round and round like hams hanging in a smokehouse. The soldiers and civilians stood wide-eyed and silent but the Modoc women screamed and cried. After a time that seemed to Billy like an eternity, the convulsions stopped. The last great Modoc chief was dead and a proud Native American culture was essentially wiped from the face of the earth.

All the surviving Modocs in Jack's band, which totaled about one hundred fifty, were loaded onto boxcars and shipped to Quawpaw Reservation, Oklahoma.

Chapter Thirty-Seven

—— OCTOBER 3, 1873 ——

Fort Klamath, Oregon
Following the execution York walked with Billy and Rattler back to the barracks. Many other soldiers loitered around the gallows as members of the press and civilians asked question and sought souvenirs. All of the whites seemed to be caught up in a carnival atmosphere.

When York's scouts sat down in the barracks there was only silence for several minutes. Then York tried to make the best of a bad situation. "Look at it this way, men. At least it's over now. We can all get on with our lives."

John Rattler looked at York with piercing eyes and an angered expression. "White man see no justice. No over, blind man," Rattler said with clinched teeth as he walked out the door with a bundle in his hands.

Rattler sat on the steps and opened the canvas bundle. There were two Colt .44 revolvers in the bundle. Rattler began dismantling and cleaning them even though they were not dirty.

York turned to Billy and spoke in a quiet voice. "It has to be over; what else could they want?" York said as if he doubted his own argument.

"That Colonel Davis is the devil himself," Billy said shaking his head. "I watched him; he loved it. He enjoyed seeing those men suffer."

"Yes, I have to say that Colonel Davis does enjoy killing," York acknowledged. "Billy, you're going to have to keep an eye on Rattler. Don't let him do anything stupid."

"He's mighty upset over what happened. You know that don't you, Billy?" York asked him.

"Yeah, damn it, I know it. I don't feel so good myself," Billy responded.

York left Billy and Rattler to themselves while he went to check on their horses. When he arrived at the headquarters building he noticed Mr. White from the War Department and Von Schlyke standing at the front of the building engaged in a conversation with Captain Hurtsell. Von Schlyke was very animated and rambling on frantically in a mixture of German and English. Hurtsell was giving instructions to four rough-looking civilians. The four men nodded as if they understood everything then left.

"Zee samples must be taken fresh!" Von Schlyke screeched at Hurtsell.

York pretended to go in another direction, then ducked between the headquarters building and a storehouse. From there he tried to follow the three men but it was getting late and he soon lost them as they moved beyond another building.

York went on to the sutler's store and stopped back by to check on Rattler and Billy. The two young men sat in the dark in silence. York sat with them for a while but then he began to worry. He thought of Rattler's words and his past experience with the Cherokee tracker. The three had been inseparable friends for years and York decided that Rattler had the best instincts of any man he'd ever known.

"That's what makes him a great tracker," York whispered to himself.

There was something in the actions of Von Schlyke and White that worried York. He thought again of what Rattler had said, then repeated it aloud to himself. "No over, blind man."

York decided that he should try to find out what they were up to so he returned to the headquarters building and began a search. He crept from building to building finding nothing. He encountered two soldiers talking to reporters and politely interrupted them. "Say, men, I've got a message for Colonel Davis. Do you know where I might find him?"

York smiled as one them answered.

"Yeah, I think he and Captain Hurtsell are over at that new tent," the man said as he pointed into the darkness.

York looked across the fort yard to a distant corner where a large tent had been erected. There was excessive light beaming from within. The young lieutenant walked toward the horse corral, then circled around to the back of the large tent. As he approached he could hear noises and chatter. There was some clicking and clanking of metal. Then there was laughter followed by a cheer from those inside.

York crept closer while looking in both directions. It was clear that he was undetected when he reached the back of the tent. He slowly moved closer until he could press one eye to the tiny gap between the tent flaps.

York gasped in absolute horror. He clapped his own hand over his mouth to keep from screaming aloud. The young lieutenant's face contorted and the color drained from his face. He broke into a cold sweat, watching as if transfixed, unable to move.

Von Schlyke stood over the corpse of Captain Jack as he carefully worked a saw through his neck. Colonel Davis stood by with a bottle of rye in one hand and a cigar in the other.

"Hurry up, don't ya know how to chop an Injun's head off?" Davis said boastfully. "Give me that damn saw; I'll show you how to deliver a savage's head." Davis set the whiskey down and pushed the little scientist out of the way.

Davis scoffed at Von Schlyke as he took the saw and began roughly hacking through the difficult neck tendons and neck bone. When he was finished he grabbed Captain Jack's head to pull it free from his desecrated body. A small piece of tissue remained uncut as Davis pulled at the head. He relaxed his grip, then jerked the head free, tearing the last piece of tissue connecting the great chief's head to his body.

Standing in the middle of the oversized tent was Colonel Davis holding up the bloody head of Captain Jack. Davis was obviously intoxicated as he paraded around the tent holding the head like a trophy. Captain Hurtsell and Mr. White stood by laughing while Von Schlyke screeched frantically.

"General Sherman wanted his head! Well, by God, here it is!" Davis roared.

Von Schlyke chased Davis around the tent with his arms outstretched. "Zee sample must not be damaged!" he screamed as he approached the drunken officer trying to get the head back. "Dees will lead to zee most important discoveries in all history."

Von Schlyke was dressed in a white surgeon's apron, which was tightly fitted around his body. Captain Hurtsell and his civilian thugs just watched and laughed. Congealed blood stained his hands and the front of his apron. The drunken Colonel Davis laughed as he handed Captain Jack's head back to the Von Schlyke.

When the head was passed Captain Jack's face was turned directly to the end of the tent where York stood watching. York grimaced as he looked into Captain Jack's twisted face. His eyes were locked open and his face was frozen in an eternal expression of pain and agony.

Von Schlyke took Jack's head and placed it in one of the large pickle jars that York and his men had carried from the coast. After the head was in the jar, Von Schlyke filled it with formaldehyde and sealed it. He took the jar and placed it on the table in the center of the tent. There was a cheer from the spectators as the macabre act was completed.

Von Schlyke then turned back to the table where the body of Black Jim lay beside the headless corpse of Captain Jack. The man instructed his assistants to hold the man's shoulders while he began to saw into the Modoc warrior's neck. The same procedure was followed while removing the head of Schonchin John.

York recoiled in disgust while still holding his hand over his mouth.

He stumbled back a few feet and moved away from the tent. He began to throw up but he struggled to stay as quiet as possible.

York fought for composure as he returned to the tent and peered inside again. There were now three jars sitting on the table with Modoc heads floating in formaldehyde. Meanwhile the spectators chatted while Von Schlyke cut off Boston Charley's head. When the head was fully separated, Colonel Davis approached and took it from the scientist holding it by the hair. He held the head up with one hand while globs of congealed blood dropped onto his uniform.

"That'll teach 'em savages to mess with Colonel Jefferson C. Davis from the great state of Indiana! These savages got what they deserved. Kill 'em, ever damned one, I say," Davis shouted.

Hurtsell looked over at the little German and laughed aloud. "Hey, Von Schlyke, ain't ya worried about that sample bein' damaged?" They all laughed and watched the little scientist scurry around the tent.

Von Schlyke placed Boston Charley's head in the fourth jar, then approached the jar with Captain Jack's head in it. He leaned over and placed both hands on it and began to caress it like a man might a beautiful woman. He looked into the tortured eyes of Captain Jack and whispered to him in German.

"Hey, White, I think your scientist friend is in love," Hurtsell said with a laugh.

When the job was completed and the head placed in the last jar, four lifeless faces stared back at them from the table.

York started to leave his spying position but something held him there. He thought the ghastly work was done, but then his eyes caught Von Schlyke leaning over a wooden crate. The mad scientist was removing something from the crate but York couldn't see what it was. When the baron raised it, York saw that it was a fifth jar, just like the others.

York was puzzled. There were only four men hung. He was sure of it. He'd witnessed the entire affair. Why were there five jars? he wondered.

Von Schlyke placed the fifth jar on the table beside the others then turned to speak. "Now vee must complete zee samples. Where is zee female of royal blood?" the little German asked. "Vee *must* have zee female!"

"Don't ya worry yerself none, little feller, she's on the way. It's a long trip from Yreka. Hurtsell's men will have her here soon," Davis said as he left the tent.

At first York didn't understand what he'd just heard. What female? What royal blood? Why did they go to Yreka? Suddenly the realization struck him. "Oh, my God! Royal blood! It's Loma! They're after her head!" York said to himself.

He turned and quickly slipped away from the tent. He tripped over a tent rope and stumbled. His mind whirled with confusion. Tears came to his eyes as he thought of Billy and his plans to marry. What could he do? How could he stop them?

York ran to the barracks and rousted Billy and York from their bunks. He ushered them into a corner where no one could hear. The young officer tried to talk but words would not come. He began to sob uncontrollably as he looked at Billy in the semi-darkness.

"Oh God, Billy," he said as he began to cry again.

York turned toward Rattler, then dipped his head as if in shame. "You were right, John; it's not over."

"Please, Yorkie, you're scaring the hell out of me. What the hell is going on?" Billy asked.

"Listen to me, Billy, you've got to control yourself. Colonel Davis will kill you like squashing a bug if you give him a chance," York said with his voice now under control.

"That little German scientist is crazy. The samples he's after to put in those pickle jars are people's heads. I found them in a big surgeon's tent out toward the rear of the post. These butchers have cut off the heads of Captain Jack and the other Modocs." York's voice began to crack again.

"What?" Billy replied, as if he thought York was the one who was crazy. His mind strained to sort it all out.

"It's true, Billy, I saw it with my own eyes. But that's not the worst of it." York began to cry again as he said it. "Oh God, Billy, they want royal blood. I think they're after Loma."

Billy looked at York in a state of total astonishment. He looked at Rattler and his expression turned to one of disbelief; he then looked back at York. "What could they possibly want with her?" Billy asked as his own voice began to quiver.

"Billy, they want her head. I think they're going to kill her and cut off her head," York said quietly. "These insane people want Indian heads of royal blood. I heard Von Schlyke say it; they want a female head to complete their samples. That little German said it had to be a female of royal blood. Loma is Captain Jack's sister."

"Oh God, they know she's Captain Jack's sister?" Billy said as if he still held out hope that the nightmare wasn't real.

York hung his head. "It's true, Billy, I saw it. I heard it myself."

Without warning, Billy dashed to the trunk beside his bed. He threw it open and pulled out a revolver and charged for the door. Before he was halfway there he was slammed to a stop. John Rattler delivered a severe blow to his stomach. Billy doubled over and dropped to the floor.

"No rush bear without scout first," Rattler said with a cold firmness.

"He's right, Billy. We've got to think of something," York said. "Where is Loma?"

"She's at home, I think. She's at the Roseborough's house in Yreka," Billy said.

"I'll bet she's not there now," York said.

"Maybe she still there. Maybe not," Rattler said while his mind churned. "Billy, get horse; get Loma. Lieutenant, get horses, saddles. Meet on Lost River at natural bridge. I find tent."

"Yeah, Billy. I think you better make a run for it. Take Loma and go. I'll mislead them. I'll tell them you went to San Francisco," York said. "I'll get horses, supplies, and a pack horse. You meet us at the natural bridge."

Chapter Thirty-Eight

—— OCTOBER 4, 1873 ——

Fort Klamath, Oregon
John Rattler opened his arms to the sky and stared at the partial moon. He took off his shirt, then knelt to the ground. His right hand swept across the earth snatching up black soil, which he began to rub across his body. He scooped more dirt in one hand, then drew stripes across his face with two extended fingers. Rattler slowly raised his eyes to the heavens and began a low chant in his native Kituhwa. It was a Cherokee funeral chant that he had learned as a child. John Rattler turned his lean body to the east and raised both hands into the air again as he spoke softly. He stood again and stared at the silver night sky, waved his arms from side to side as he continued to chant and turn in circles. After several complete rotations he twisted to a stop again facing east.

"I come to you soon, my father."

Rattler finished his personal version of a traditional Cherokee ceremony. He was at peace with himself and totally resolved. He would do what had to be done.

Rattler returned to the barracks and retrieved his two Colt .44 revolvers. He opened the trunk beside Billy's bunk and pulled out two more pistols that belonged to Billy and York. He strapped on two pistol belts.

He checked the ammunition in each one, then tucked two of the guns into the holsters on either side. One more was tucked under the leather belt and the fourth was carried in his hand. He found a short, sturdy stick and shaped the end with his little Cherokee knife. With thin leather straps he mounted and tied a rifle bayonet to the end of the stick. He slid the improvised weapon through a belt loop, then he slipped out into the darkness of night.

The Cherokee tracker had already located the surgeon's tent and he knew that Hurtsell and Von Schlyke were still there. He had a fresh horse already saddled. Rattler led the animal all the way around the yard until he came up behind the surgical tent. He hid the horse in the brush with saddle in place. Well over an hour passed with Rattler constantly watching and waiting. A large freight wagon appeared with two civilians driving and many uniformed guards riding alongside. Two more civilians rode in front of the procession. The wagon was covered with white canvas concealing any cargo.

Captain Hurtsell came out to meet the wagon as it came to a halt in front of the tent. Von Schlyke dashed around to the back of the wagon excitedly. He peered inside as the men began to dismount. The four civilians went around to the back of the wagon and dragged a large bundle wrapped in a carpet off the back of the wagon. Rattler watched as two men carried the bundle inside.

The Cherokee tracker's heart sank as he watched them pull Billy Long from the wagon with his hands bound behind him and a rag tied across his mouth. His face was blackened and distorted with lumps swelling in several places. Dried blood covered his face and part of his dirty uniform. The two guards dragged him inside the tent; then Hurtsell and Von Schlyke went inside and closed the flap. The soldiers remained outside dispersing through the camp. A few soldiers sat around a small fire chatting amicably.

Rattler slipped past the only two guards standing near the tent. He worked his way around to the back of the tent where he could peek inside. He watched as the men unrolled the carpet bundle. The tough Cherokee tracker ached inside when he saw them pull the covers off the beautiful Modoc princess Loma. Tears came to his eyes because at first glance he thought she was dead, but then he saw the gag over her mouth and realized that her hands were tied behind her. They placed her on the large surgical table, then stepped away.

Billy sat in the corner bound and gagged. His head was bowed, and his muffled cries could not be heard. He struggled to get free but could not.

Von Schlyke hovered over Loma and talked to her softly in German. He brushed her cheek and stroked her hair as a groom would his bride. He put on his apron as Hurtsell and the four civilians joked of what they would like to do to her.

After the little scientist had finished tying his apron he returned to her, then looked back at Hurtsell. "Zee sample is perfect," he said with a smile.

Loma's eyes darted about in absolute terror. She turned her head enough to see Billy seated in the corner. Their eyes met briefly and Billy wailed through his gag as tears poured from his eyes. He struggled violently against his ropes. One of the civilians approached him and kicked him in the chest.

"Quit yer whinin'. You won't be hurtin' fer long," the man said, laughing.

Rattler knew time was running out. He circled to the front of the tent just as the two guards there had separated. In complete stealth the Cherokee tracker grabbed the first guard, slapping his hand over his mouth while simultaneously slipping the bayonet forcefully between his ribs. He drove the bayonet at a forty-five degree angle upward towards the man's center, killing him instantly. There was a slight sucking sound but then only silence. He dragged him back a few feet out of immediate sight, then circled around to the other side of the tent where the second guard stood by the wagon. Rattler killed him in the same fashion. It was over in a matter of seconds with only a thud and a wheeze.

The young Cherokee went back to his spying position and peered into the tent. Von Schlyke was standing beside a surgical table talking to

Loma. He opened his case and pulled out a surgical saw and several odd-looking knives. Next he reached into his case and removed a bottle and held it up to the lantern. He picked up a small towel and held it with one hand while he poured ether into it with the other hand.

He looked down at Loma and whispered softly, "It vill last only a moment."

The little German instructed two of Hurtsell's civilians to hold Loma's arms and shoulders. He wanted her still so that he could press the towel over her face.

The two men rolled Loma onto her back, and held her while Von Schlyke soaked the towel with a deadly dose of ether.

Suddenly the civilian standing closest to the back of the tent gasped; then there was a sucking sound as a loud thump was heard. His eyes bulged; then the man fell forward with a rifle bayonet protruding from his back. Behind him stood a Cherokee warrior with a .44-caliber revolver in each hand.

In a fraction of a second the two pistols exploded with fire and smoke. The loud reports deafened all within. Gun smoke clouded the space.

The first shot hit Captain Hurtsell on the left side of his nose blowing out the back of his skull upon exit. The combined blast of brain matter, bone, and blood hit the man standing behind him in the face, temporarily blinding him. The second shot hit the little German in the left side of the chest traveling all the way through and striking one of the civilians holding Loma in the abdomen. The other two civilians had scarcely removed their pistols when both were shot down.

Rattler rushed to Loma and pulled off her gag, then untied her; she rose to a sitting position. Her eyes opened wide as she stared at him in a near state of shock.

"Untie Billy," he said calmly as he went to the front of the tent and peered out. He could see the soldiers scrambling to their feet and searching for their weapons.

Rattler turned back to Loma and Billy and pointed to the back of the

CHAPTER THIRTY-EIGHT

tent. "Go that way. Horse in brush," he said as he turned and slipped through the flaps on the front of the tent.

Two soldiers were approaching cautiously as Rattler came out. At first they weren't sure what they were seeing. By the time they had raised their weapons Rattler was already firing. The soldiers had long rifles, which made shooting at close quarters difficult. One of them managed to get off a shot but Rattler shot them both down. A third soldier fired a shot from beside the freight wagon but it missed. Rattler hit him in the neck with a .44 round.

The Cherokee scout searched for a saddled horse and found one with a soldier standing just a few feet away. Rattler fired and missed and the soldier also fired and missed. The man threw down his rifle and took off running. Rattler discarded the two empty pistols he was holding and ran to the horse. He looked about as he tried to control the frightened animal. He untied him and mounted as two more soldiers ran forward firing. Rattler turned the horse with one hand as he pulled another pistol from his holster and fired, but the horse's movements caused him to miss. He fired three more rounds hitting one man in the leg and sending several others diving for cover. Rattler turned his horse and rode away toward the back of the tent, where he found Loma and Billy scrambling toward the horse tied in the brush.

Billy ripped the plant from its roots and leapt onto the large gray animal. He reached down and pulled Loma up onto the horse behind him.

"Go! Run!" Rattler yelled as he turned back toward the scrambling soldiers.

Billy kicked his horse and dashed away into the predawn darkness. Loma held on tightly as the horse bounded away. Billy could hear more shots popping behind them. From experience Billy knew that some were pistol shots but others were from rifles. Billy rode south toward the rendezvous point as fast as he could.

Loma shouted in Billy's ear as the horse moved through the darkness. "What about Rattler? We must help him," she cried into the wind.

"We can't help him. I don't have a gun and we're supposed to meet him at the natural bridge. Yorkie is waiting there with fresh horses and supplies."

Billy covered a reasonably safe distance but continued in caution as he was forced to slow down. They still had several miles to go and Billy worried about wearing out his horse with such a heavy load and hard riding. He kept to side trails and shortcuts that hid them from prying eyes. The sun was rising as they approached the border between Oregon and California. When Billy was close to the natural bridge he swung left circling back to the rendezvous point. He did not see York anywhere, but then he heard a whistle coming from a juniper thicket up on a hill above Lost River.

Billy rode up the hill where the two exhausted riders climbed down from their horses. York and Billy grabbed each other while Loma fell to the ground emotionally and physically exhausted.

"Oh, thank God! You made it!" York said as if he thought he'd never see them again.

"Rattler shouldn't be too far behind us if he made it," Billy said with anguish in his voice.

It was the first time Loma had gotten a good look at Billy's face since Hurtsell's men had beaten him. His blackened and bruised face looked horrible and she climbed to her feet and embraced him. "What did they do to you?" she screamed as she held his face gently between her hands.

Loma and Billy embraced each other as Loma sobbed quietly. Tears formed in Lieutenant York's eyes as he watched the two lovers.

"I will never let you out of my sight again," Billy vowed. "I love you more than life itself. I'm gonna marry you."

"Billy, I gotta tell you, we're in serious trouble here," York said. "The whole U.S. Army is going to be looking for you. If Rattler doesn't get here soon we'll have to leave. We have no other choice."

"I know that, Yorkie, but let's give him an hour. John Rattler is mighty good; he just might make it," Billy said with unconvincing optimism.

Billy and Loma took water and ate beef jerky while they waited. Loma wet a rag and wiped the dirt and blood from Billy's face. He had a large bump and cut over his left eye that was still seeping blood.

"What's wrong with the soldiers? Why do they want people's heads?" Loma asked as she nursed her lover's face.

"It's some kind of crazy science. I heard 'em talking about it while I was in the wagon," Billy said as he looked north hoping to see a single rider. "It's called phrenology. That loco German scientist says he can solve all the world's problems by studying the right skulls. They were going to kill you and cut off your head." Billy broke down crying as he said the words.

"How could such people call us savages? What kind of army takes people's heads?" Loma asked York.

"I don't know but I can tell you that they're the savages, not you."

York turned to continue looking for Rattler when he saw a rider coming in the distance. "It's a rider!" he shouted.

"Oh God, please let it be him," Billy said, his lips quivering.

Billy jumped to his feet and stared into the distance. They watched carefully as the rider got closer and closer.

"He's leaning in the saddle," York said with concern in his voice.

Billy's emotions began to overcome him. He began to cry openly as they watched Rattler get closer. "If he's hurt bad I'm going back there and kill every damn one of those crazy bastards," Billy said between clinched teeth.

"You stay here. I'm going down there," York told them as he mounted his horse.

Lieutenant York rode to the bottom of the hill and met Rattler as he approached. What he saw startled him. Rattler's left ear was blown off and hanging by a piece of flesh. York could see where Rattler had packed it with dirt to stop the bleeding. His right arm hung limp and a bloodied bandanna was tied around it. The lower left side of his shirt and the top of his pants were also dark with blood.

York took the reins of Rattler's horse and led him to the top of the hill while Rattler did his best to hold on. Billy met them and caught Rattler as he rolled from his horse. He grunted in pain as Billy laid him on the ground. His skin color looked strange and his face was covered with beads of sweat and dirt.

York secured the horses and the three of them gathered around Rattler. "Oh God, what have they done to you?" Billy said between sobs.

Loma wet a rag and began to wipe the Cherokee's face. Rattler looked up at the two lovers and smiled.

"You make it," he said quietly.

"Oh hell yes, we made it, thanks to you, my brother," Billy said in obvious gratitude. "We got to get you well. We're gonna get away from here."

"Yorkie?" Rattler said as if he didn't see him. "Many soldiers come… too many. No stay here."

All of them were crying now except Rattler. He continued to address York directly. "Go to lava beds; soldiers look for three horses." Rattler's breathing labored as he struggled to talk. "No leave sign, no track in lava. Yorkie, take three horses out of lava, go west. Billy and Loma go east, brush tracks. Soldiers follow Yorkie. Billy and Loma go home." Rattler coughed between breaths.

"He's right, Billy, they don't have anything on me. When they catch up with me I'll tell them you must have gone to San Francisco. But you know they'll be after you for the rest of your life," York said as he looked back at Rattler.

"Billy…no let them take my head," Rattler said in a weak voice.

"No! I swear to God, I'll kill them all first," Billy told him as he continued to cry quietly.

Rattler moved his good arm toward his waist and reached inside his pants. He removed the little Cherokee knife that his father had given him as a little boy. He looked at it briefly, then handed it to Billy. Billy briefly examined the beautiful decorations then looked back as Rattler began to speak. "Take knife, my brother. Go to Big Snowbird Creek. Follow creek to big fork; my father there. Solider look for Indian named

CHAPTER THIRTY-EIGHT

Rattler and white man named Long. Take my name; tell father you his son now. Show him knife. He know then, this be true."

"No, ya ain't gonna die. Hang on now, John, please," Billy begged as he watched the dimming light in Rattler's eyes.

"Tie in blanket; bury me on Big Snowbird Creek. Soldiers no get head," Rattler said softly between shallow breaths. "You John Rattler now. You Snowbird Cherokee." Rattler forced a slight smile.

The Cherokee turned to Loma and smiled again. "You have many Rattler babies."

John Rattler took Billy's hand and squeezed it softly.

"My brother," Billy said as he watched his friend close his eyes.

Rattler's breathing slowed further until there was none. York put his hand to his chest and felt for a heartbeat. There was a slight flutter, then it stopped. John Rattler, the greatest tracker the West had ever known was dead.

Billy burst into tears, pulling Rattler up and holding him in his arms. He rocked back and forth wailing as he moved. Loma put her arms around Billy and cried with him. York knelt beside them and wept openly.

Several minutes went by when York finally spoke up. "Billy, we can't stay here. You've got to go."

"I'm going back and kill as many as I can before they kill me," Billy said firmly.

"No, Billy, please come to your senses. You've got to do what Rattler said. If you don't, you're betraying him. He gave his life so that you and Loma could live and marry. Don't mess that up," York begged him.

Billy began sobbing again. Then he looked at Loma and shook his head. "Let's take him home to his father." His voice cracked but there was resolution in his tone.

Billy and York checked horses and supplies while Loma tied a cloth then a blanket around Rattler's body with strips of leather. When the work was completed York took some of the supplies off the packhorse and he and Billy laid Rattler's body across the horse and tied it securely.

"Remember, Billy, if you meet soldiers tell them that the man in the blanket died of some mysterious disease and they won't get near you. He will start stinking terribly; they'll be afraid of catching something," York said.

When all preparations were made, they rode down the hill toward the lava beds. York led Rattler's and Billy's worn out horses while Billy and Loma rode fresh horses with the packhorse tied behind them. They went into the lava beds, then dismounted. After an extended and arduous hike they came to a point in the lava flow where York stopped and looked at Billy.

"I guess this is it, old friend," York said as he looked to the west toward the setting sun. "You must go that way, I have to go west. They'll eventually pick up my tracks and follow the three horses. But all they'll find is a washed up lieutenant who'll be leaving the army as soon as his enlistment is up." York smiled.

The two men looked at each other as York extended his hand. Billy took it, then began to cry again. He embraced York and held him for a brief moment. Then the two separated. York mounted his horse while taking the rope holding the other two.

"Good-bye, Loma. You do what John said; have lots of babies," York said with tears forming in his eyes again.

"Good-bye, Yorkie," she said through her own tears.

Paul York turned to Billy and smiled. "Good-bye and good luck, Billy."

Billy looked at him for several seconds with a strange expression that York was unsure of. Billy lifted his head and held it high, then sucked in a deep breath. He looked at York and spoke loudly with determination in his voice. "My name is not Billy. I am John Rattler, Snowbird Cherokee." He gestured to Loma, then took his horse's reins. He looked at York for the last time, and saluted. He smiled briefly, then turned around and started marching east, with the sun to his back.

Chapter Thirty-Nine

—— SEPTEMBER 3, 1915 ——

Graham County, North Carolina
Whips of fog circled up from the coves deep in the Smoky Mountains as the sun popped through the broken clouds. It was late morning on Big Snowbird Creek and Loma had a small cook-fire going in the little cabin. The coffee was boiling and bacon sizzled on the old black skillet. The Modoc princess turned Cherokee rolled dough for pan-cooked biscuits while Billy and Wosley washed in the nearby stream. When the meal was ready she called in the two men and five grandchildren who were present.

There was barely room as all eight of them crowded around the small wooden table. Billy said a traditional blessing, which was followed by a loud "amen" from Wosley. The happy family ate heartily as Wosley and Billy continued their discussion.

"I'm glad you told me of your experience, Billy. It's a story that needs to be told. Most people are good but when bad ones show up we should expose them even if it seems too late," Wosley said as he cut his bacon with a dull knife. "I just wish John Rattler could be with us for a day so he could see all of this. He would have wanted to meet your seven children and all the grandchildren too."

"Yeah, he would have liked that. Down deep he was a true family man, ya know," Billy said.

"Yes, and Yorkie too. He is so pleased to know I found you. He wouldn't tell me the story himself. He said I had to find you and get it directly from you and Loma. It's a miracle you made it."

Wosley pulled his watch from the little pocket and held it by the gold chain while he studied it. "It should be sometime this afternoon before Stringfield gets here. Maybe he'll be here by mid-afternoon."

"I'm going to be real sorry to see you go, Wosley. I've kinda taken a likin' to ya," Billy said with a chuckle.

"I really hate to go; this is such a beautiful place. In fact it's the prettiest place I've ever seen," Wosley added. "But I've got to get your story out."

As the sun peaked overhead a slight breeze began blowing in from the west. Billy and Loma sat on the front porch while the grandchildren played in the yard. The rustling of leaves imitated a whispering voice among the dense hardwoods. There was a call from the edge of the forest as the old Confederate colonel came into view at the bottom of the hill. Colonel William Stringfield was on horseback along with five other men as they approached the cabin.

Billy and Wosley stepped off the porch as the men rode up the hill. Four of the other men were obviously natives but the fifth was a white man. Billy took the bridle of Stringfield's horse and held him steady while the old soldier dismounted.

Stringfield and Billy exchanged greetings while Wosley spoke in Kituhwa to the Cherokee escorts.

The other man dismounted and walked over to join the others. Stringfield took him by the shoulder with his left hand while gesturing to Billy with his right.

"May I present Mr. Paul York from the great state of Massachusetts. I believe you may have met in the past," Stringfield said with a broad grin spreading across his face.

Billy took one look into the man's eyes and recognized that it was

CHAPTER THIRTY-NINE

true. He was looking at the man who'd saved their lives. They had not seen each other in decades. Billy rushed to him and embraced him. He pulled away after a brief moment and looked back into his face. Both men were overcome by emotion; neither uttered a word for an uncomfortable moment.

"My God, it is you!" Billy said.

Loma came out of the house and rushed to York clamping him in a tight embrace.

All three of them had tears of happiness in their eyes as they looked over each other up and down.

"Honestly, I never thought I'd see you again," Billy said as he began to smile.

"Thank you, Mr. Wosley. If you hadn't tracked him down we would have never seen each other again," York said.

Billy shook his head in disbelief as he looked at his old friend.

"I didn't think I'd ever see you either," York said.

Colonel Stringfield and the Cherokee escorts took time to eat and rest while Billy and York talked constantly.

When the visitors had been fed and rested Colonel Stringfield announced that it was time to leave. York was staying for a few days but Wosley was leaving. Wosley took time to thank Loma especially, for all her help and the good food. He and Billy shook hands for the last time. All the men mounted their horses and turned to leave but Billy shouted after them. "Thank you, Mr. Wosley, for bringing us together."

Wosley turned in the saddle and yelled back at him. "Think nothing of it, my good man."

The two old soldiers and Loma reminisced through the afternoon. They laughed and joked just like in the old days out west.

Billy looked at Loma with admiration as he described how they had come all the way home carrying Rattler's body in a sewn-up leather bundle. They crossed over mountain ranges and rivers as they traveled all the way from California to North Carolina.

"We worried more about passing people than crossing rivers or mountains. We saw soldiers in just about every town we came to for a while. Sometimes people would approach and we'd shout to them that my brother had died of sickness. For a while the smell was somethin' awful." Billy laughed as he remembered. "They'd take one look at that leather sack thrown over the packhorse. Then they'd start walking backwards real fast.

"I'd go into a town here and there just to get some supplies. But for the most part we stayed away from folks."

York stood and stared toward the window, then looked over at Loma and Billy, his mind gone to another time and place. "I know he's up there somewhere, Billy. Would you be willing to take me to see him?" A small tear formed in the corner of his eye as he spoke the words.

Billy turned to Loma and smiled.

"I think John would like it very much if you came to see him. You've come so far, old friend," Loma said as she looked at him affectionately.

Loma rose and stood beside York holding his right arm. She turned to Billy and spoke softly. "Let's go now, Billy, there's still light."

The three old friends hiked a short trail through a grove of large chestnut trees to a little hill overlooking Big Snowbird Creek. As they came over the hill York could see a sizeable vertical stone sticking out of the ground. York picked up his pace, then came to a stop in front of the stone.

"Hello, John Rattler! I've come to see you, old friend. I expect to join you in another world soon." York got the words out, but as soon as he'd finished he broke down sobbing.

Loma rushed to him and pressed her face to his chest. Billy just watched them for a moment with his lip quivering. Loma turned back to Billy and took his hand; then she reached back and grasped York as she stood between the two of them facing the stone. Billy began to whimper at first, then sobbed openly as he dropped to his knees. The other two immediately knelt beside him. Loma looked up at the stone and spoke through a wave of tears.

"He saved my life," Loma said, her voice shaky.

"I was in two armies and in several wars but I never fired on another man. I reckon Rattler did all the shootin' for me that I'd ever need," Billy said

York looked at Billy and Loma as he wiped tears from his face. He took a deep breath as he regained his composure. Then his voice found its strength and he declared boldly, "We should never forget one thing as long as we live. If it had not been for John Rattler, the greatest tracker there ever was, Loma's would have been the fifth skull.

Historical Perspective

It has often been said that truth is stranger than fiction. The documented history behind this story is just such an example. There was a fifth skull. The U.S. Army did put a known murderer in charge of a murder investigation, trial, and hanging. U.S. Army Colonel Jefferson Columbus Davis of Indiana did murder his commanding officer. The same Jefferson C. Davis did oversee the mutilation and beheadings of Modoc Indians.

The Fifth Skull

In the year 2004 I published a book called *The Secret of War: A Dramatic History of Civil War Crime in Western North Carolina*, which was a recounting of my family's oral history. The research on that book led me to investigate the conduct of certain military officers and their postwar careers. Tracking Colonel, once brevet Major General, Alvan C. Gillem led me to California and the Modoc War. What I found there startles and disturbs me to this day. I knew Gillem was an unethical and incompetent officer but the man who took his place, Jefferson Columbus Davis, was much worse.

The Modoc Chief Kei-in-to-poses, known to whites as "Captain Jack," was an honorable man who led the Modoc people to a peaceful coexistence with area settlers. In exchange for that he was betrayed, abused, and in the end murdered as an outcome of a fraudulent trial.

In 1872 the U.S. government had taken everything the Modocs had and forced them onto a reservation with another tribe. It was a larger tribe that had been traditionally the enemies of the Modocs. After countless abuses and betrayals Captain Jack took the Modoc people back to their homes on a tiny, nearly worthless piece of land in northern California. They only asked to stay in their homes and live in peace. The refusal of the U.S. government to allow them this tiny place to live led to the Modoc War. Captain Jack held off the U.S. Army for months with only about fifty men, while burdened with many women and children.

Kei-in-to-poses or *"Captain Jack,"*
last free chief of the Modoc tribe
PHOTO COURTESY OF NATIONAL ANTHROPOLOGICAL ARCHIVES

In 1873 U.S. Army General E. R. S. Canby, commanding officer of the Department of the Columbia, came to northern California to negotiate a peaceful solution to the problem. The result was a series of strange occurrences that have never been fully explained.

Colonel Gillem was the field officer in charge of the troops, yet he seems to have done little to aid the peace effort. Gillem sat in his tent while the Modocs were killing General Canby. After his death, Colonel Jefferson Columbus Davis of Indiana replaced General Canby. Davis was a known murderer at the time. The appointment was made by then General of the Army, William T. Sherman.

Captain Jack was betrayed by one of his own, captured, placed in irons, and, along with five other Modocs, charged with murder. He and the other men were placed at the mercy of Davis. A sham trial in the form of a military commission was conducted to make it seem legitimate. It was the sole decision of Davis that the Modocs should not be allowed any legal representation. No reasonable defense was presented.

Except for one man the military commission consisted of soldiers who had been fighting the Modocs and losing.

Was Captain Jack guilty of the murder charge?

It is the opinion of the author that Captain Jack was wrongfully convicted of murder. He was not the man who killed Canby. Captain Jack was probably guilty of conspiracy, assault and battery, and attempted murder, but not murder. The man who killed Canby was a Modoc named Bogus Charley. In any event, one must consider that what the Modocs did might have been considered acts of war under the circumstances. White men did not honor a truce. Why should they expect the Modocs to do so?

Eyewitness testimony available from the time proves that Captain Jack did not cause Canby's death. He fired a shot that apparently hit Canby on the right cheekbone "under the right eye." The bullet must have glanced off because Canby was still very conscious and alert after the shot hit him. He started running but was soon tripped by Bogus Charley. Bogus Charley then stood over Canby, pulled his head up, and cut his throat. It was Bogus Charley who delivered the deathblow to Canby, not Captain Jack. This account can be found on page ninety-one of *The Indian History of the Modoc War* by Jeff C. Riddle.

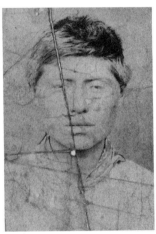

Bogus Charley, Modoc warrior
PHOTO COURTESY OF NATIONAL ANTHROPOLOGICAL ARCHIVES

One murderer takes care of another.

It is a documented fact that Bogus Charley stayed in Gillem's camp the night before General Canby was killed. There is no doubt that Bogus Charley was part of the group of Modocs who pressured Captain Jack into going along with the killing of Canby. There is also clear evidence that Bogus Charley went straight to Davis when he deserted Captain

General E. R. S. Canby, U.S. Army

PHOTO COURTESY U.S. ARMY MILITARY HISTORY INSTITUTE

Jack. It was Bogus Charley, known to speak good English, who acted as the go-between for Davis and Jack's surrender.

When it came time for Davis to try to hang people all the power was his. He exempted Bogus Charley from prosecution. His excuse for doing so was because he had cooperated in the surrender. He may have cooperated more with Davis than the record indicates. This is the same Modoc man who had cut Canby's throat. Bogus Charley walked free just as Davis did when he murdered his own commanding officer in 1862.

When I began researching this story I followed the evidence from California to Washington, D.C., and Suitland, Maryland. Some of the secrets behind this story are still held in "restricted" files at the National Anthropological Archives in Suitland, Maryland. The skulls of Captain Jack and the other Modocs were turned over to the Smithsonian Museum of Natural History sometime between 1898 and 1904. I searched for them and found that they had been returned to Modoc

Colonel Jefferson Columbus Davis, U.S. Army

PHOTO COURTESY NATIONAL ANTHROPOLOGICAL ARCHIVES

family members in 1984. When I inquired about the fifth skull, which is not mentioned in any of the early documents from the period, they admitted that there was one. The fifth skull is described as being a female, her identity unknown. J. O. Skinner delivered her head to the Army Medical Museum. Skinner was a civilian contract surgeon for the army at the time. He was probably present and or assisting while Surgeon Henry McElderry removed the heads from the four Modoc warriors. Skinner was rewarded for his gruesome service with a regular army officer's commission in 1874.

In response to my inquiry Mr. Bill Billeck, program manager for the Smithsonian Museum of Natural History, acknowledged that there was a fifth Modoc skull. On June 2, 2008, he wrote: "The fifth individual is female and died of disease near Lost River in 1873 and her name is not known." The Army Medical Museum turned over the skulls to the Smithsonian in the late nineteenth century. The only information available is what the army placed in the record. The record indicates she died of disease but since the other skulls were taken "unethically," I do not accept this claim. A known murderer at the time, Jefferson Columbus Davis was still in charge. Although I have nothing but the presence of a known murderer and a nameless dead female to support my theory, I suspect this girl's head was also taken "unethically." I have included the photo of another Modoc girl named Mabel Hood. The photo gives us some idea as to what the unnamed female might have looked like before Davis and his team cut her head off. This photograph also gives us some idea of what poor Rosie Jack, Captain Jack's daughter, would have looked like had she lived. She died at Quapaw, Oklahoma, just a few months after they arrived there.

Prior to my research on Jefferson Columbus Davis there were a few serious studies of the man. One of those was *A Thesis: Brigadier General Jefferson C. Davis*, by Bruce V. Sones. He does an adequate job of describing the murder of General Nelson by Davis. But he leaves out other crucial negative items including the details of the Ebenezer Creek affair. Sones was a U.S. Army major seeking a graduate degree when he wrote the thesis as a degree requirement.

A book on Davis was published in 2002. Entitled *Jefferson Davis in Blue: The Life of Sherman's Relentless Warrior,* it was written by Nathaniel Hughes Jr. and

Mabel Hood, Modoc girl
PHOTO COURTESY OF NATIONAL ANTHROPOLOGICAL ARCHIVES

Gordon Whitney. They covered the details of the murder well. If one reads those details it is not hard to see that Governor Morton and other Indiana men who were enemies of Nelson were engaged in a plot to excite Nelson's temper. They expected Nelson to be armed. I believe the plan called for Davis to murder Nelson; then Morton and the others would claim self-defense. It appears that Davis was acting on behalf of Morton and others who wanted Nelson dead.

For that reason, Governor Morton went straight to Washington, met with President Lincoln and Secretary Stanton, and lied to them. Morton was actively engaged in a cover-up. This behavior is understandable since the governor might have been implicated had Davis ever been brought to justice on the murder charge. It is interesting to note that nine years later General Canby would be murdered by use of the same kind of plan involving the same Jefferson Columbus Davis.

It is my personal opinion that Jefferson Davis murdered General Canby. The Modocs were his murder weapons. He was probably paid by Jesse Carr to do the deed. Once the Modocs were blamed for the murder it was easy to wipe out the tribe.

Hughes and Whitney don't even mention the Modoc head-chopping incident. They do give a good accounting of a lot of records and correspondence regarding Davis at the time. This work will give one the impression that except for the fact that he was a murderer, possibly a mass murderer, he was an "effective" soldier. You might also get the impression that he was able to get some men to follow him, that he was a "leader." These attributes can also be applied to Adolf Hitler.

It is the opinion of the author that after the Nelson murder, no future commanding officer would dare write negative reports on Davis. After all, the last commanding officer in a conflict with him ended up dead. Davis was a real killer and they all knew it. Such men are sometimes considered valuable in times of war.

I suspect that General Sherman liked having Davis on his team because he knew he could give him dirty jobs to do. He knew Davis would do anything. Now that I know Davis was with Sherman on his famous march through Georgia, I have a better understanding of why several generations of Southerners were taught to hate Sherman.

The Union Prison at Camp Douglas, Chicago, Illinois

Readers who encounter my work may have a hard time believing that the Union prison at Camp Douglas was worse than the infamous Confederate prison at Andersonville, Georgia, but it was. A relatively new book by George Levy, former assistant attorney general for the state of Illinois, contains the proof. Levy states that the Union prisons were worse because they practiced murder and torture as routine matters. No such things were done at Andersonville.

This story is so unpleasant that I don't expect people to believe it at first. I would direct all readers to Levy's excellent work on the topic: *To Die in Chicago: Confederate Prisoners at Camp Douglas 1862-65*. Levy's book was the source for the History Channel's feature program on the topic, *Eighty Acres of Hell*, which first aired in 2005. There were so many documented horrors at Camp Douglas that it was difficult to include them all in one story. In my book all of the accounts of torture, murder, and abuse really did happen to individuals at Camp Douglas.

Colonel Benjamin J. Sweet, U.S. Army
PHOTO COURTESY OF U.S. ARMY MILITARY HISTORY INSTITUTE

The Lost Boys of the Confederate Junior Reserve

On February 18, 1864, the Confederate Congress passed a new conscription act that called all young men on their seventeenth birthday. Approximately two hundred boys from the western counties of North Carolina were called with the initial draft in April 1864. About one hundred twenty of them were captured at Camp Vance and sent to Union prisons. Most of the records pertaining to Confederate soldiers from North Carolina have no listings for the captured boys. We do not know who most of them were. Buried somewhere deep in the bowels of our National Archives in Washington, D. C., are the records for groups of Confederate soldiers labeled as "Unassigned Conscripts." The records for some of them may be found there.

As for those who escaped capture that day most of them were reassigned from the Ninth Battalion of Junior Reserves to the First Regiment of Junior Reserves. Most of these boys served honorably through the end of the war. One of them, William Preston Lane of Henderson County, was elected captain and assigned to Hoke's Division defending eastern North Carolina from Sherman's invading Union army.

When Hoke needed time to maneuver he called up two companies from the First Regiment of Junior Reserves and ordered Captain Lane to lead a charge into the enemy line. Lane led what must have been one of the last Confederate charges of the American Civil War near Kinston, North Carolina, on March 9, 1865. When it was over Captain Lane lay shot through the chest. Somehow he survived his wounds and returned to Henderson County, where he was a prominent citizen for the remainder of his long life.

Captain William Preston Lane, Henderson County Confederate, First Regiment of Junior Reserves; at Confederate Veteran's Reunion, Asheville, North Carolina, approximately 1910

PHOTO COURTESY OF CHRISTY CRAFT

Terrell Garren at the grave of Rosie Jack, Quapaw, Oklahoma, June 2004

Terrell Garren on the Cherokee Reservation at Snowbird

Terrell Garren in the lava beds, northern California, 2006

General Sherman with officers, including murderer Jefferson C. Davis
PHOTO COURTESY OF THE U.S. ARMY MILITARY HISTORY INSTITUTE

Troops on parade at the lava beds at the time of the Modoc War
PHOTO COURTESY OF THE U.S. ARMY MILITARY HISTORY INSTITUTE

About the Author

Terrell T. Garren was born in Asheville, North Carolina, on July 5, 1951. He graduated from T.C. Roberson High School in 1969. He earned his BS and MA degrees from Western Carolina University in Cullowhee, North Carolina. Garren is a U.S. Army veteran and a former public school administrator. He was administrative assistant to former U.S. Rep. James McClure Clarke and served during three congressional terms. He has been a commercial writer and is the author of *The Secret of War: A Dramatic History of Civil War Crime in Western North Carolina* (2004) and *Mountain Myth: Unionism in Western North Carolina* (2006). He currently resides in Henderson County, North Carolina.

CONTACT INFORMATION
Terrell T. Garren
P.O. Box 15162
Asheville, NC 28813
terrellgarren@bellsouth.net